H. C. Harding

**Axtell and Allerton**

H. C. Harding

**Axtell and Allerton**

ISBN/EAN: 9783337371258

Printed in Europe, USA, Canada, Australia, Japan

Cover: Foto ©Andreas Hilbeck / pixelio.de

More available books at **www.hansebooks.com**

# Axtell and Allerton.

THEIR PERFORMANCES AND SUCCESSES,

TOGETHER WITH

# A BIOGRAPHICAL SKETCH

OF THEIR OWNER,

# C. W. WILLIAMS,

To Whom the Fame and Prosperity of the Western Trotting
Horse is Justly Due.

BY H. C. HARDING
WEST LIBERTY, IOWA.

CEDAR RAPIDS, IOWA:
DAILY REPUBLICAN PRINTING AND BINDING HOUSE.
1892.

# TO THE READER.

The writer of this little volume does not claim to be a writer, as the term is generally used. The intent has been simply to give in as few words as possible an account of the wonderful success of C. W. Williams, the acknowledged peer of all horsemen. There are but few people that do not admire a good horse. Therefore a history of the greatest pair of trotters that ever lived, together with a sketch of the man who bred and developed them, should be of interest. If this end has been attained, the writer will feel that his effort is not in vain.

# Axtell and Allerton.

## CHAPTER I.

### C. W. WILLIAMS.

Charlie Williams came to Iowa when quite young with his father, and settled on a farm near Jesup. Iowa, only a short distance from Independence. The elder Mr. Williams not being overburdened with the good things of this world, and having a large family dependent upon him, it was necessary that each one should do his part. Therefore we find "Charlie", as he was called, thus early in life doing whatever came in his way that would bring in an honest dollar, and if there was not a dollar in it, he was just as ready to secure one-fourth of the amount. In this way he was taught when but a boy the great and all important lesson of self reliance, without which no man is likely to succeed.

When still young, he undertook to learn telegraphy. He took a position in the Illinois Central office at Jesup, and in a short time, mastered the art of handling electricity, and was given the night office at that place. After filling the position acceptably for a time, he gave it up and accepted a position with the same company at Independence, Iowa. He filled this place for quite a while. But this kind of employment did not suit him. Being a man of ability and possessed of ideas of his own, it is not strange that he sought some occupation that would be more congenial,—in short, a business in which he could make his own plans, and in a great measure, dictate his own terms.

After severing his connection with the Illinois Central, he embarked in the grocery business at Independence. He operated this business for a time, and then sold it out. McDonell Bros. are doing business in the room at present.

His next venture was working for A. J. Barnhart of Independence, who was engaged in the creamery business and handled eggs. Mr. Barnhart was a warm friend of Charlie Williams, and stood by him in all of his business enterprises, which favor Mr. Williams returned later on.

After working for a time for Mr. Barnhart, he went to Ossian, a small town some distance north of Independence, bought a creamery and went into business on his own account. After getting the business under way, he conceived the idea of furnishing butter to private families in the larger cities. Pursuant to this idea, he put up a sample package of butter on which was printed his advertisement, went to Chicago and canvassed the city, leaving the sample of butter and an egg at private residences, at the same time informing the good housewife that he would call next day to take her order. This proved to be a gratifying success. He was enabled to obtain forty-five cents per pound for his butter, and the demand so far exceeded the supply that he was obliged to send to Decorah for butter to supply his customers.

While conducting this business he was impressed with the idea that he might be able to make something by handling hogs, there being an abundance of butter-milk, as a result of the butter making. In accord with this idea he built an immense hog house, filled it with hogs and was doing quite a profitable business. However, the introduction of the hog business was the beginning of trouble for Mr. Williams at Ossian. The people complained that the swine were not as sweet smelling as good fresh butter, and as a consequence the city council branded Mr. Williams' *hog pen* a nuisance, and he was compelled to discontinue the business.

While living at Ossian, Mr. Williams became somewhat interested in the trotting horse. He was the possessor of a buckskin trotter, which he raced with the boys at county fairs, and if reports are true, the buckskin was oftener behind the money than otherwise. However this may be, the determination to own a trotter, and a good one, was strong in Mr. Williams. It was while attending the fair at Independence with this same buckskin trotter, that Mr. Williams bought Gussie Wilkes, the dam of the great and only Allerton.

The Messrs. H. L. & F. D. Stout, of Dubuque, had a number of horses at Independence in charge of a Mr. Kelly. They were making arrangements to ship the stock home, and Mr. H.L. Stout went to Independence to look the stock over. The result of the inspection was the rejection of a number of horses and mares, with the instruction to Mr. Kelly to sell them for what they would bring. Among these offcasts was Gussie Wilkes. Mr. Williams' attention was called to the mare by a young man by the name of John Hussey, who was working for him at this time. After looking the mare over Mr. Williams asked Mr. Kelly the price. Mr. Kelly said seventy-five dollars. Mr. Williams without more ado said, "I will take her." Lou, the dam of Axtell, was bought sometime previous to this. For her Mr. Williams paid one hundred and twenty-five dollars.

Here, without parade or show, were sold these

two offcast mares. The Messrs. Stout did not consider them worth keeping for breeding purposes, although breeding and developing the trotter was their business. Little did Mr. H. L. Stout think when he instructed Mr. Kelly to sell these mares for what they would bring, that they were destined to become famous; their produce would astound the world and not only make their owner a millionaire, but make the then unimportant village of Independence the Mecca of America for the breeding and developing of the grandest of all horses—"The American Trotter."

The spring following the purchase of Lou and Gussie Wilkes, Mr. Williams sent them in charge of John Hussey to Kentucky to be bred, selecting William L. to mate with Lou and Jay Bird for Gussie Wilkes. The mares were left in Kentucky until foaling time so that they could be bred a second time while there. On the 26th day of March, 1886, at Lexington, Kentucky, in Tom Montague's Omnibus barn on Short street, Lou foaled a brown horse colt. On the 31st day of March, 1886, at the same place, Gussie Wilkes also brought forth a brown horse colt.

The mares and colts remained in Kentucky until about the first of July, when Mr. Hussey brought them home to Independence.

The colts at this time were not above the average in point of good looks. In fact, the one afterwards named Axtell was a very ordinary looking bit of horse flesh.

Mr. Williams' plan of naming the colts was, as they were the first colts foaled his property, to name them alphabetically, hence the names Allerton and Axtell. The foal of Gussie Wilkes, Allerton, and the foal of Lou, Axtell.

The winter following the purchase of Lou and Gussie Wilkes, Mr. Williams sold out at Ossian, remarking at the time that if they did not want him at Ossian, he would not stay. He moved to Independence and embarked in the butter and egg business again, and about this time purchased the old fair grounds, containing forty acres, with the intention of using it for a breeding and training farm. Onto this ground he moved the obnoxious hog pen which had so sorely troubled the good citizens of Ossian. He pulled the hog pen to pieces, loaded it on the cars, shipped it to Independence and built a barn from the lumber. This barn is still on his premises, and is being used this season by Mr. John Hussey as a training stable.

He continued in the butter and egg business right along, looking after his colts, but did not do anything toward developing them until the latter part of July after they were one year old. John

Hussey broke the colts to harness and drove them a little through the fall and winter.

As there have been so many stories afloat re lating to the price that Mr. Williams offered to take for Axtell, it, perhaps, will not be amiss to state that Mr. Williams did offer to sell him for three hundred dollars to a gentleman who was shipping a load of mares to Nebraska. This gentleman thought the price too high and offered two hundred and seventy-five dollars for him, which offer, as is well known, was refused. It was but a short time after, however, that it would have required thousands to buy him.

In the spring of 1888 when the colts were two years old, Mr. Williams commenced to drive Axtell in earnest, and John Hussey drove Allerton. It was not long until they made the discovery that both of the colts could "trot some." Some time during the summer or fall of 1888, Mr. Williams sold his butter and egg business to Mr. H. E. Palmer, and devoted his whole time and attention to his horses.

Axtell showed wonderful speed in his two-year old form, captured the two-year old record, and was the talk all over the country among horsemen. His record of 2:23 at two years was considered wonderful. Axtell was talked about and the time for him to trot as a three-year-old anxiously

looked forward to by thousands of people. He
had become so noted that Mr. Williams was able
to make arrangements to give exhibition miles at
race meetings and fairs. He came onto the turf
in his three-year-old form and astounded all horsedom. He awakened a new interest in the business.
People became frantic as the great colt reduced
his record time after time, finally gaining the
stallion record of the world; the fastest record for
any stallion either trotting or pacing, living or
dead—2:12. At the close of the season Mr. Williams sold Axtell for one hundred and five thous-
and dollars ($105,000) the highest price ever paid
for a horse up to that time.

After the sale of Axtell Mr. Williams was enabled to embark in the horse business in a manner
which undoubtedly exceeded his fondest expectations. He decided immediately to build a mile
track of the kite shaped variety, the plans having
been produced by Clark's Horse Review. Mr.
Williams owned at this time about two hundred
and twenty acres of land, but it was not so well
suited to his purpose as was a strip of land adjoin-
ing his property, containing one hundred and
twenty acres. For this Mr. Williams paid ($12,-
000) twelve thousand dollars, and commenced at
once to build his track. Thus in less than one
month after selling his great colt Axtell, he is

busy at work constructing this new odd shaped track.

It seemed that people were either envious of Mr. Williams' grand achievements thus far, or they possibly believed what they very freely expressed to the effect that Williams would part with his money as rapidly as he made it: foolishness for him to put so much money into a track, buildings, &c., so far from any of the large cities; horsemen would not attend a pumpkin show in the northwestern corner of Iowa, &c., &c. Mr. Williams had already shown himself capable of attending to his legitimate business, and he continued to work at his track at intervals through the winter when the weather would admit.

Early in the spring of 1890, he had a small army of men at work grading the track, building amphitheatre, barns and stalls, and an almost innumerable number of things to be done before Rush park, as the new grounds had been named, would be in condition to receive the public.

Mr. Williams had advertised his first meeting to take place in August, and on the first of January preceding had opened a series of trotting and pacing purses of the uniform value of $2,000 each, making a grand total of $40,000 in all to be contested for, the entrance fee to these purses being five per cent, just one-half charged by all other associations up to this time. It can be readily understood why the classes filled so handsomely; a splendid mile track, princely purses and only one-half the entrance fee charged at other places. it is not to be wondered at that horsemen took the chances and went. And above all Mr. Williams guaranteed every dollar, and his guarantee was good.

The great meeting came on and with it thousands of people from all over the land to see Williams, his wonderful track, the great Allerton, in short, to behold the cream of the trotting and pacing world. The meeting was a success in every sense of the world. People came away pleased with the quantity and quality of the sport, praised the people of Independence for the royal manner in which they entertained, for be it remembered Independence is but a little city of four thousand inhabitants, and when twelve or fifteen thousand visitors sought shelter and food it was necessary that almost every house should take its quota of boarders and lodgers, which they did in a manner entirely to the satisfaction of the visitors.

Horsemen were enthusiastic over the great kite shaped track; said it was the fastest track in the world; their horses could work on it, and not get sore, and altogether Independence *beat them all.*

The next meeting was in the latter part of October. This was intended principally for a record meeting, and the purses were of the uniform value of $300. This meeting was a surprise to many. There were several hundred horses on the grounds, almost two hundred and fifty entered in the class races and hosts of them to obtain records. This meeting was also a success in every way. The writer was privileged to witness the grandest performance by a team at this meeting, that it has been the lot of any man to witness. I refer to the mile trotted by Justina and Belle Hamlin, owned and driven by C. J. Hamlin, of Buffalo, New York. a pleasant old gentleman, seventy years of age.

The mares came on the track hitched to a speeding wagon and were driven a mile the wrong way of the track by Mr. Andrews, Mr. Hamlin's trainer. They were stopped near the judge's stand, and the starting judge announced that Justina and Belle Hamlin would start against 2:15, the world's record for a team made by them. Mr. Hamlin mounted the wagon, drove them around the loop and scored for the word. He nodded at the first attempt and away they flew. As they speeded down the long stretch driven by this white haired grandfather, it looked the easiest thing imaginable to drive a team of trotters. They reached the quarter in 32½ on to the half in 1:04½. As they rounded into the stretch the cold strong wind met them. and men said. "They will never do it," but on they came. never faltering and were at the three quarters in 1:39¼, and the shout went up, "They'll do it! They'll do it!". But at the distance Justina made a break, and from many a heart there came "Oh! too bad! But see! She's caught! They'll make it yet!" and as they swept under the wire at a two minute gait the applause was almost deafening. Mr. Hamlin, after driving a short distance, turned and came to the judges stand. when the time was announced 2:13¼, and there went up another great shout and loud cries of "Hamlin! Hamlin!" rent the air. In response Mr. Hamlin went up into the judge's stand, took off his hat. and made a bow. The starting judge, after announcing the time, made the following statement:—

"Ladies and gentlemen, taking into consideration all of the facts in connection with the wonderful performance which you have just witnessed, it is by far the greatest event of the age, in connection with the trotting business. Mr. Hamlin bred and owns the sire, the dams and granddams of this pair of mares." At the conclusion of this meeting the curtain drops on the scene at Rush Park for the season of 1890. Let us see what has been accomplished. Two great meetings have been successfully engineered and besides being a decided success financially, the track has to its credit the following: Of the seventeen two-year olds that entered the 2:30 list in 1890, eight of them did it on this track, and finally, one eighth of all the horses entering the 2:30 list in 1890. got their records on Mr. Williams' great course.

Is there not good reason for the claim that it is the fastest track on earth? It would not be unreasonable to suppose that the flattering success which rewarded the proprietor of Rush Park in his first attempt as a race meeting manager should have inspired him with confidence to attempt still greater things. To be convinced that he did attempt and accomplish it, we have only to look over the reports for the season of 1891. He claimed dates for three meetings; one in July, one in August and one in October.

The August meeting was intended to be the great meeting of the year, and such it proved to be; not only the great race meeting of the year, the greatest of the age. The immense sum of $90,000 was offered to pay the purses and specials. As a special attraction for this meeting a purse of $5,000 was offered for five-year-olds. The entries in this race consisted of four of the greatest race horses in the world, viz: Nancy Hanks, 2.14: Margaret S, 2:12½; Navidad, 2:22½ (did not start): and Allerton, 2:13. This was a great drawing card

2

for the meeting, people making the journey of thousands of miles to witness the battle of the giants.    This proved to be the greatest race ever witnessed, as thousands upon thousands will bear testimony.

To give some idea of C. W. Williams' untiring energy and unlimited resource, the following taken from the American Trotter, dated Aug. 13, 1891, tells the story:  "It has been suggested that in case of rain, the sport of the August races will be marred to a great degree, but we will say that preparations have been made that will defy the elements, unless it rains continuously. Within three hours after any ordinary storm the track will be fit for racing, and the following is the *modus operandi* that will bring it into shape:  A large number of sponges that will hold nearly a pail full of water each have been secured, and immediately after a rain, boys will go over the track with those sponges and take up all the water that is collected in pools.    After this a large flock of sheep that is owned on an adjacent farm will be turned on the track and driven around several times; the horses and colts will be turned on from the pasture and also driven around, after which light harrows will be put to work and jogging on the track will begin.    Within three hours the track will be fit for racing.    Those living in ad-

joining cities will please bear in mind that a storm
in the morning does not mean a postponement of
the races. The big meeting is bound to be a success, rain or shine."

It was not necessary to use the sponges and
the sheep, as the weather was all that could be desired. Who now can say that Williams' success
is luck! Is it not rather the unparalleled business
ability which he possesses?

The October meeting coming so late in the season it was hardly to be expected that it would be
anything out of the ordinary. But, strange as it
may seem, horses and horsemen flocked thither by
the hundreds, and Independence was again taxed
to the utmost. But she was equal to the occasion
and entertained her guests in the usual cordial
manner. There were thirty-six class races, with
purses of $200 in each and every race. There
were a large number of entries in all of the classes.
The meeting was a grand success and again Rush
Park settles down to every day life.

On Feb. 8th, 1892, Mr. Williams sold at
Woodward and Shanklin's sale at Lexington, Ky.,
a number of horses, among them Barnhart, a full
brother to Allerton, and Drextell, a full brother to
Axtell. These horses did not sell for as high
prices as was expected; at the same time $15,000

for a five-year-old stallion and $7,500 for a wean-
ling would be considered a handsome price by
most men. But, as compared with their aristo-
cratic relatives, they were certainly very cheap.
Men will tell you that it is all in the blood. If
they are bred to trot, they must trot and they
would just as soon breed to an undeveloped sire as
to his developed brother. Here is an instance:
Allerton vs. Barnhart; Axtell vs. Drextell. Both
Allerton and Axtell command a service fee of
$1,000. If the full brothers are just as good to
breed from, they were almost given away. With
the opening of the new year, we find Mr. Williams
with untiring zeal pushing forward and making
arrangements for the coming season. He has advertised another great meeting to be held in
August, 1892. Two full weeks, commencing Aug.
22nd, and closing September 3d; $200,000 in
stakes, specials and purses, a number of them of
the value of $10,000, the entrance fee ranging
from one to five per cent. Mr. Williams says
that "the earning capacity of the trotter must be
increased." He says that "we are producing ten
high bred colts now to one five years ago." Mr.
Williams is surely doing his part towards increasing the earning capacity of the trotter, if a light entrance fee is of any benefit in that direction. He
has shown to the public his ability to manage race

meetings, and to do it in a manner calculated to inspire respect and confidence. We therefore confidently expect to witness the greatest meeting of all in 1892.

## CHAPTER II.

### INDEPENDENCE AND RUSH PARK.

Independence, Iowa, is the county seat of Buchanan county, and is located forty miles northwest of Cedar Rapids. Iowa. It is a beautiful little city of about four thousand inhabitants, surrounded by a splendid farming and stock growing country. The town is of more importance than a great many places that boast of a larger population. The Wapsie River flows through the town, dividing it almost in the center, furnishing excellent water power, which is utilized for milling purposes, and might be turned to account in various ways, such as manufacturing, etc.

Another thing that gives Independence an advantage in a business way, is the location here of the largest of the state hospitals for the insane, a structure erected a few years since at a cost of over one million dollars, and having a capacity of about nine hundred inmates.

But the one thing which has made Independence famous was the founding and operating of

Rush Park, which is located one-half mile from the business part of the town, on the west side of the Burlington, Cedar Rapids and Northern Railroad. The farm contains three hundred and forty acres of land, all utilized in pastures and paddocks. except the part on which the track is built. Ten large barns on the place afford. with the stalls at the track. accommodation for four hundred horses with a box stall for every animal. The barns are lighted with electricity, and a system of water works furnishes water in the barns and on the racing grounds.

Near the larger barns and on an elevation commanding a fine view of the track, is Mr. Williams' residence. erected at a cost of fifteen thousand dollars. It contains all of the modern conveniences, is elegantly furnished. and also lighted with electricity.

Near the kite shaped track is a good half mile track. which Mr. Williams contemplates covering and heating with steam, to be used for training purposes through the winter.

It is also his intention to put in an electric railway which will connect the two depots (the Illinois Central and the Burlington. Cedar Rapids and Northern). running through the business part of the city, thence to Rush Park, and on to the Asylum which is beyond.

When these improvements are completed, Independence will have the best facilities for training the year through of any city on the continent, and as they already have the "fastest mile track on earth" may they not reasonably expect that Independence will become the very *center of the trotting world.*

## CHAPTER III.

### AXTELL AS A TWO YEAR OLD.

In his two-year-old form, Axtell made his first appearance on the turf at Keokuk, Iowa. August 9th. 1888. In the race for three-year-olds, mark you, for three-year-olds, he won the race in the second and third heats, last heat in 2:31¼, distancing the field. There is one thing that it would be well for the reader to note. Williams has been called "lucky." Take particular notice of all his dealings in the two years immediately following this date. and then draw your own conclusions. There is not much doubt but that it was a surprise to the other starters in this race. to not only be beaten by a horse a year younger than theirs. but to be distanced, and by this colt from the northern part of the state, was pretty rough. But facts are stubborn things; Axtell reached the wire before they could get by that hated piece of red bunting. and there was nothing to do but stand it, and own that this northerner was a good one. On August

11th, 1888, Axtell started at Keokuk, against his own record, 2:31¼, but failed to equal it; he trotted in 2:32¼.

His next start was at Chicago, at the North-western Breeders' Meeting, August 25th. As a matter of course his Keokuk performance was fresh in the minds of the people, bu tthe question is, is he a trotter that will train on and trot on, or was this an accidental flight of speed that he might never be able to accomplish again. An answer to this question, Williams and Axtell were not long in giving. At Washington Park, Chicago, Aug. ust 25th. 1888, Axtell started against his record. 2:31¼, and trotted the mile in 2:30¼. Mr. Williams was not satisfied with this, and after about forty minutes between heats, he sent him another mile. which he finished in grand style in the phenomenal time of 2:24¾. This performance fell like a thunderbolt upon breeders and horsemen in general. It was at this time that men began to ask who this man Williams was. Where did this colt come from? I believe there is some fraud about this thing. etc.. etc. Such expressions as the above were freely indulged in. Such talk as, that Williams was favored by the judges in the matter of time. was currently reported, anything but to believe that Axtell was a truly great horse. And why was this? Simply because he had not

emanated from some wealthy breeding establish-
ment, because his dam was not a $5,000 pur-
chase with all of the incrosses and outcrosses and
breeding or business attached, with a tabulated ped-
igree that dated back to the thoroughbred stallion
that tore loose from Pharaoh's chariot when he
was crossing the Red Sea in pursuit of the fleeing
children of Israel. In short, Axtell's breeding was
not considered fashionable. Well, we will see
what a man and a horse can do toward making
these things come their way. It may not be
generally known that there was some exceptions
taken to Axtell's mile at Chicago in 2:24¾. The
facts are as follows: After he had finished the first
mile in 2:30¼, Mr. Willams made known to the
judges that he would drive Axtell another mile,
and accordingly when the prescribed time arrived.
Mr. Williams was on the track with Axtell ready
to go, but was informed by one of the judges
that he must wait until Madam Some-body-or-other
got through with a saddle horse exhibition. Consequently he was compelled to wait some fifteen minutes, making in all a wait of about forty minutes
between heats. This would not have made any
difference had Axtell trotted in about the same
time as the former heat, but when it came to flashing under the wire in 2:24¾, thereby capturing
the two-year-old record, it was a little too much.

and the judges concluded that they did not know whether this could be legally called a record. No fault of Mr Williams that he did not get away on time. Yet they talk about the validity of the record. However, it mattered but little, as subsequent events will show. This is simply thrown in to show what kind of help Mr. Williams was getting from judges to push himself and his now famous horse to the top. Axtell's next start was at Minneapolis, Minnesota, August 30th, 1888, special purse $500, against time 2:26¼. Axtell won in 2:24. Still a little better. It makes but little difference now what the decision of the judges at Chicago was. The plucky Hawkeye colt can now boast of a record ¾ of a second faster than the one made there, and it looks as though he might still lower it; he is in good condition, and when he makes his fastest miles, it is without any great exertion. It seems to be natural to the colt to trot, and when he gets at it right, it is apparently but little trouble. From Minneapolis, Axtell is shipped to Des Moines, Iowa, to attend the Iowa State Fair and take a part in the races. He is entered in the race for three-year-olds, purse $580. He won it in the first, third and fourth heats, dropping the second heat, time 2:43, 2:34:, 2:35¾, 2:38. This was an easy victory, the time made not being so fast as the first race that he started in.

From Des Moines, he goes home to Independence to take a little rest, and attend a meeting at the county fair.   Here he is given a purse of $100, providing he beats 2:31¼, this being his record on a half mile track.   The Horseman, dated September 20th, 1888, says; . "At the county fair at Independence, Iowa, on September 14, the two year old colt Axtell, 2:24, owned by C. W. Williams, of Independence, was driven a mile for a special purse to beat his best record on a half mile track 2:31¼.   When he was brought on the track it was raining, but he finished the mile in 2:30, without a skip, trotting the home stretch in the face of the blinding rain and strong wind.   A running horse started to accompany him, but after the first quarter fell far behind.   The half mile track there is slow, and twenty-five feet over length."   On September 19th, 1888, Axtell and his breeder, owner, trainer and driver, C. W. Williams, are at Cedar Rapids, Iowa, attending the Iowa Breeders' Meeting.   The event is ably related by a correspondent to the *Horseman*, from Burlington, Iowa, dated October 11th, 1888, as follows:

"Preparatory to lowering his record of 2:30 on a half mile track, Mr. Williams appeared with his pride, Axtell, the king of two-year old colts, and he made his first attempt, trotting a mile in 2:30¾.

with two breaks. He was accompanied by Alpha, a
black mare, owned by H. L. and F. D. Stout, of
Dubuque, Iowa, and driven by Mr. Kelly. Mr.
Williams, having three trials to accomplish the
difficult task, appeared later for the second attempt
amid applause from the great crowd congregated
to witness the performance.    After scoring twice
he got away, trotting the quarter in 38 seconds,
the half in 1:13¾, three-quarters in 1:53 and the
mile in 2:27¼, which was pronounced the greatest
performance ever made on a half mile track, by
old and experienced judges who witnessed the
performance.    He did not appear disturbed in the
least while trotting the last quarter at a 2:21 gait.
Axtell is undoubtedly the most perfect trotter
that has ever appeared on the turf.    The total
weight of his four shoes is twelve ounces, four
ounces in each of the front, and two ounces in
each of the hind shoes, wearing nothing but scalp-
ing boots, and they are used merely as a precau-
tion.    The above performance was regarded
equivalent to 2:20 on a good mile track, by professional horsemen, as the track was slow.

After his victory over time at Cedar Rapids,
the next mention we see of the young monarch is
at St. Louis, Mo.   If he made an effort against
any particular record here, I have not been able to
find it, either in Wallace's Year Book, or in the

files of The Horseman. The following appeared in the last named, in the issue dated October 4th, 1888.

The writer, after making mention of a number of horses, speaks of Axtell as follows: "Axtell looks brighter, and altogether he appears to be in better fettle than when at Washington Park. Whether he will be sent a fast mile at the fair I do not know; I presume not, though if the day be favorable, and the track in good shape, he may reduce his record. The track at present is anything but fast, being very soft and cuppy in many places, and it needs working badly, but for all that Axtell went a very easy mile yesterday in 2:27$\frac{1}{2}$, which is as fast as any of the horses could make it, free-for-all contestants included."

The next and last place that Axtell is exhibited as a two-year-old is at Lexington, Kentucky, the far famed Blue Grass State. Kentucky, has been noted for time almost immemorial as the home of fine horses. It seems strange that she should appeal to the comparatively new state of Iowa for an attraction to draw the masses to her great race meeting. But such is the case. Did I say that it was strange? Truly it seems so, but the old adage "True merit always wins," is only being verified again as it has been thousands of times. We know that this was rather a hard blow on our

Kentucky brethren, this landing Iowa a winner
in the horse business in a single heat.   But we
must acknowledge that you have shown rare good
judgment in adopting this phenomenal youngster,
and thereby creating good feeling, and eventually
reaping some of the benefit, which must necessar-
ily follow.

Lexington, Ky., October 8, 1888; prize, silver
cup; Axtell against time, 2:26¼.   Axtell won;
time 2:23.

The Horseman, dated October 18, 1888, says:
"Axtell went a second mile accompanied by a
runner.   He went to the half in 1:10, and finished
in 2:23, true and strong.   It was a grand performance, unparalled except by the mile of Wildflower,
and when it is considered that Axtell has been
shipped all over the country, trotting on half mile
tracks, and has never had the advantage of a day's
training by a professional trainer, his mile is a
marvel."

Hold on, brother.   Do you think in your honest heart, that there is another man that could have
done better with Axtell, than C. W. Williams, of
Independence, Iowa?   True he has had but little
experience, but did it never occur to you that this
man was a natural conditioner and driver?   I will
agree with you, there are hosts of men that know
more about the chicanery of race driving, for of

this Mr. Williams, does not profess to know anything, in fact I do not know that he professes to
know anything at all, but to use the vernacular of
the old darkey, he just "goes and does it." Do
not be deceived. If a man is not a natural driver,
you may just as well undertake to give an im-
ported Clyde a record of 30, as to try to make of
him a successful trainer and driver.

On November 1st, Axtell started again at
Lexington against his own record of 2:23. but
failed to equal it, trotting the mile in 2:28¼.

This ends Axtell's public work as a two-year-
old; he now retires into winter quarters with the
two-year-old stallion record 2:23. He has been
the wonder of the season, coming from obscurity.
and at a single bound landing in the very front
rank. Think of him at Keokuk, his very first attempt in company, starting with a field of three-
year-olds, himself at that time under size. distancing the party, and lacking but one and one-quarter
seconds of getting into the Charmed Circle.

Then again at Des Moines. starting against
another field of three-year-olds, and winning at
will.

During the season he has trotted nine miles
against the watch, the most stubborn of contestants, winning six and losing three. but he did

3

not fail to win at every meeting when he was started.

Won his race at Keokuk; lost the mile against time. At Chicago, first mile against time won; second, won. Won his race at Des Moines. At Independence won against time. Cedar Rapids first mile lost. second won. Minneapolis against time, won. Lexington, against time, first mile won; second. lost.

It can be seen at a glance that while he lost three miles during the season, he was winner at all meetings when he was started, and now we will not see more of the great colt until summer comes again. There is not much doubt but that he will make some very fast miles around the warm stoves in club rooms and in livery barn offices, and such like places, but we doubt very much whether the most sanguine will be prepared for his wonderful performance as a three-year-old. We will now leave him snugly ensconced in his cozy winter quarters at Independence until the racing season comes again.

## CHAPTER IV.

### AXTELL IN HIS THREE-YEAR-OLD FORM.

The first that we see of Axtell in 1889, is at Cedar Rapids, Ia., June 27th, at the summer meeting of the Cedar Rapids Trotting Asociation, where he is to trot against time, 2:26¼; purse, $500. The following taken from the Horseman, dated July 4, 1889. will give some idea of the esteem in which Axtell was held. "The card of the day was the wonderful three-year-old colt, Axtell, to beat the three-year-old record over a half mile track. When Mr. Williams and Axtell made their appearance, they were greeted with a hearty cheer. After a little warming up, the Wonder scored for the word. and as it was given, a hundred watches were started. He reached the quarter in 35 seconds, on he flew to the half in 1:08½, and he finished the mile easy in 2:21¾. As he jogged back to the stand, the immense crowd arose in a body and gave three cheers for Axtell and Charlie Williams.

It is universally conceded by horsemen that Axtell could have beaten 2:20, had his owner so

desired.   I predict that Axtell will be the sensa-
tional horse of the year, and I fully believe he can
beat the three-year-old record.   He was driven to
a forty-five pound Frazier sulky, it being the first
time that he was ever hitched to it." A wonderful performance, it being so early in the season,
also taking into consideration the fact that Axtell
was a stallion, and was taken from the harem and
started in a race.   His next start is at Minneapolis, Minnesota, July 2nd, special purse against time,
2:18.   Two eighteen!   Think of it.   Only a baby,
his first mile of the season in 2:21¾, and with only
five days intermission, asked to go a mile better
than 2:18.   Can he do it?   Williams must be
crazy!   He will kill the colt! and such like expressions were freely indulged in at the time, and,
by the way, bear with me and I will relate a little
incident that took place at the time that Axtell
trotted in 2:21¾ at Cedar Rapids.   I was at that
time living at Mediapolis, Iowa, and had made arrangements with Mr. C. P. Johnson, better known
as "Tip," to attend the Cedar Rapids meeting and
see Axtell trot.   When the morning of the race
came, it was impossible for me to go, but as no
such bad luck attended "Tip," he went.   I might
state here that Mr. Johnson is a horseman, his
father having owned and campaigned runners, but
"Tip," in keeping with the times, was becoming in-

tensely interested in the trotter, so that he was on
the lookout for any stray bit of information that
might be picked up, consequently when he went
to see Williams and Axtell, his eyes were open.
A few days after the meeting I met him, and he
gave me an account of the wonderful mile trotted
by Axtell. But, said he, "the strangest thing to
me is the way Williams feeds. Why, Axtell was
to trot at half past one, and I was at his stall at
eleven, and he was eating timothy hay like a plow
horse, but he came out and trotted a mile in 2:21¾,
and did it easy. Well, I thought I would go
round and see how he cools out. I don't think that
I ever saw a horse cool out nicer, but Williams surprised me again; just when he was nicely cooled,
and I thought ready for a bran mash, or a little
hay, his groom came in with all the green grass
he could carry, and threw it down to the colt;
that settled me." Well "Tip," said I, what do
you think of that kind of treatment? "What do I
think of it! Gad! What must I think? See how
how he trots!" Here can be seen the beginning
of C. W. Williams' influence on the feeding and
manner of caring for the trotter. How many
trainers were there up to this time that advocated
heavy feeding, especially hay! How many were
there that thought green grass good for a cam-
paigner! The answer is easy, very few. Young

men can very well remember the time when it was
thought if a horse by some mischance filled himself
with grass, he would not be fit to go into a  race
for from one to two weeks after.

The successful trainer of to-day has very different ideas; he favors plenty of good wholesome
food, and a little grass every day.  When did men
commence feeding this way?  Did you ever think
of it?  But to return to our hero, let us see what
the outcome is at Minneapolis.  Again we will give
the account as taken from the  Horseman of July
11, 1888.

"Axtell's performance to-day was something
wonderful.  It was a raw, cold day, the wind blow-
ing against him through the stretch.  His mile in
2:15½, stamps him the greatest colt ever foaled.
In the pool rooms last night, Axtell sold for $15;
time, $10.  At the track to-day nobody wanted
Axtell.  Taking the conditions, the day, &c., into
consideration, the odds were ten to one that Time
would win.  After scoring once he was started
for the task, and as the starter gave him the word a
hundred watches were started.  He flew to the
quarter in 33 seconds, and on to the half in 1:06, a
shout went up as the time was called.  He went to
the three-quarters in 1:40, and as he straightened
into the stretch, he was seen to waver.  Wililams

commenced to lift him. and tapped him lightly with
the whip, when he let out a link and passed under
the wire a winner in the unprecedented time of
2:15¼, not only beating the three-year-old record,
but beating Manzanita's four-year-old record of
2:16. When the colt and driver returned to the
stand, they were greeted with a hearty round of
applause. After the trial I asked some of the
prominent horsemen to give their opinion on the
day. John Splan said, had the day been good, he
would have beaten the stallion record. Knap
McCarthy thought the day two and one-half seconds
slow; Ben Walker. three seconds; C. W. Kinney,
one and one-half: C. Cattrill, one: Rody Patterson,
one; M. E. McHenry, two: Bob Stuart. two and
one-half: H. D. McKinney. two; Lee Pendal. two;
George Wilde, two: Al. Swearinger. two. H.
D. McKinney offered Mr. Williams $50,000 for
Axtell. Mr. Williams replied that it would take
$100,000 to buy him. When you take into con-
sideration this colt has only had three miles better
than 2:40, this spring, his performance of to-day
leads me to think he will trot a mile close to 2:10
this season. A. H. Simons. the popular secretary
of the St. Paul Association, ever ready to secure
the best, made arrangements with Mr. Williams
to trot for a special purse of $2,000, at St. Paul,
next week.

Well, the timothy hay and green grass did not kill him, neither did his fast mile at Cedar Rapids impair his speed, but rather seems to have brought him to an edge, and he still lives and is making more engagements; the wise ones are shaking their heads and saying, he can never do it again. All things to him who waits. Wait, brother, and we will see.

The next place selected to battle against time is Independence. Home, how Mr. Williams' heart must have throbbed within him, as the thought came to him that he would exhibit his treasure to those he knew best! Reader, did you ever raise a colt, train it to halter and to harness, care for, feed and groom it, until it came to be a full grown horse? If you have, then you know something of the feelings of C. W. Williams on that fourth of July, when he came out behind the wonderful colt, and knew that he was among friends who were taking almost the same interest as himself. Mr. Williams did achieve greater things afterward, but in the estimation of the writer, this was the proudest, most glorious day of his career. The feat to be performed at this time, was to beat the three-year-old record, 2:21¾, over a half-mile track; purse, $500. He trotted the mile in 2:20½, and did it easily. Now we are beginning to think that Mr. Williams should be satisfied; he has

gained enough laurels for one season. With a
record over a mile track of 2:15½, and 2:20¼
over a half mile track, what more does he crave?
Ah! there is a certain world's stallions record not
very far below 2:15¼ that Mr. Williams is beginning to view with some concern. As anticipated,
in the account of the Minneapolis meeting, on
July 11th, we find our champion colt trotter and
his irrepressible owner and driver at St. Paul,
Minnesota. Say! did it ever occur to you that
Axtell was a great traveler? I can hear scores of
voices answer, he certainly must be, to be able to
trot a mile in 2:15¼. Oh, certainly, but that is not
what I meant. I refer to him as a railroad traveler. In the last fourteen days, he has been
shipped about seven hundred miles, and has
trotted three fast miles. This is quite
a jaunt, and we would not feel surprised if our
baby trotter would become discouraged. But not
one bit of it; he goes out at St. Paul, and trots in
2:15½, just the same as the mile at Minneapolis.
But good judges, not the official judges, said that
Axtell trotted the mile fair in 2:15¼. However,
judges in a horse race are all powerful, and this
case was not an exception to the rule. Although
it would seem, that, taking into consideration the
rivalry which exists between Minneapolis and St.
Paul, that the latter place would gladly have con-

ceded the one-fourth part of a second, and had it said that Axtell trotted the fastest over their track. But so it is. and the record must show 2:15½.

## CHAPTER V.

### AXTELL AT CLEVELAND, OHIO.

After a rest of twenty days, on August 1st, we meet an Iowa wonder in the Buckeye state, at Cleveland, Ohio, at that time the very center of horsedom, so far as race meetings were concerned. This is the same city and the same track where the immortal Maud S. set the mark of 2:08¾, which remained untouched for so many years. Judging from the make up of men in general, don't you think Mr. Williams would feel a little shaky here. with the eyes of the whole horse world upon him? He is going to undertake to drive his three-year-old colt a mile better than 2:15½, a feat which has never been accomplished, and which in the minds of a great many people is an utter impossibility, all things considered. It would seem that an amount of confidence. and cool determination, beyond the ability of man to command. would be necessary at this time to pilot the great colt through this mile. For be it remembered. Axtell is but three years old. Mr. Williams is but an amateur driver. He was not known to the horse world until Axtell commenced as a two-year-old to show speed. The eyes of hundreds of men who had made training the trotter their life business were upon him. His methods were peculiarly his own, and were radically different from theirs, and it is not strange that they should think that Mr. Williams' career would be short. There is not much doubt but that some of these same drivers felt that in a measure this new man was infringing on their territory, as it were, and making known to the world that any man with good judgment and determination could train and drive a trotter. All this Mr. Williams possessed, and he turned it to good account. The Horseman, dated August 8th, describes the Cleveland mile as follows:

"Axtell's great mile in 2:14¾ excited the admiration of critical horsemen. Doubts were freely expressed as to his ability to equal his record of 2:15¼. It was a wonderful rating mile. The first quarter being accomplished in 33¼ seconds, and each of the others in 33¾ seconds, or as near an even mile as possible. So much has been written of him, that I will say little here, except to describe the mile. He trotted it without a skip, or a break, and I think could have gone a little faster. Any doubts as to his greatness, which existed, are now dispelled. He is simply a phenomenon, pure gaited, level headed, and even tempered, in fact, a perfect trotter." Ah! he did not disappoint the great crowd of people assembled to see him, and best of all, he did not disappoint his fond and confident owner. He has again proven himself to be the greatest horse on earth. He has set a new mark for three-year-olds, and indeed it begins to look as though he would set a mark for all horses. August 21st, we find Axtell at Chicago. Well, it will be strange if some of those Chicago sharks don't steal Axtell's speed away from him, or, still worse, steal the horse outright, and try to make Mr. Williams believe they have bought him. They are a bad set, young man. Beware! Wallace's year book says: Special purse $—: against time, 2:13¼; Axtell (3 years) B. H., by William L., time, 2:15¼; lost. While the Horseman of August 22, 1889, has it Axtell against 2:14¾; time, 1. Axtell, b. c., C. W. Williams, 2; time, 2:15¼.

It matters but little which is correct, so long as the outcome is the same. Here is an opportunity to ring in the old thread-bare ·‧I told you so." I knew those Chicago sharpers would steal something, and they have done it. But wait a day or two, and we will do business with an honest man; Honest Jim Graham, as he is called, of Biggsville, Ill. His good horse, Earl McGregor, by

Robert McGregor, and Axtell, take a tilt at it. Mr. Graham, you had a good horse, but he was raised on the wrong side of the river. To have a winner this year, he must be an Iowa horse.

Purse $—; for stallions:

Axtell (3 years) b. h., by William L., 1-1-1.

Earl McGregor, by Robert McGregor. 2-2-2. Time: 2:19, 2:14, 2:20¾.

Where are those fellows that have been shouting all summer about trials against time? Such expressions as, he is not a race horse! He never trots in a race! I believe he is a quitter, &c., &c., &c. Come, now, boys, own up! It will do you good. See those three heats; average time. 2:17½, a shade better than 2:18, and more. Axtell has again set a mark for three-year-olds, 2:14, and done it in a race. Bravo! You need not be ashamed of your horse, Mr. Graham. It was no disgrace to be beaten in such time, and as we cannot all own record breakers, let us rejoice with Mr. Williams and the trotting horse world in general. In just five days after this wonderful performance, Aug. 28th, Axtell is started at Cedar Rapids, Iowa, against time, 2:27, for a purse of $1,000, winning in 2:23; just a nice work out for him. The next day, August 29th, he is started at Independence against 2:23, for a purse of $500, and won in

2:22. Another nice work out. An easy way to make $1,500, and not hard on the horse, either. Ah! But if 2:22 was as fast as he could trot, do you think he could command these prices, and dictate his own terms? No. Axtell is now a horse with a great reputation, but he has earned it, hewn it out, and he is already beginning to reap some of the benefit. Axtell's last performance being at Independence, at home, he is given a rest, his next public performance being at St. Louis, Mo., October 4, 1889. However, during this time he is taken to Des Moines, Iowa, to attend the State Fair, but as he was suffering from a severe attack of influenza, Mr. Williams did not start him against any particular time, but simply drove him an exhibition mile in slow time. He was shown here in a glass house, or rather a stall built expressly for the occasion, with windows on all sides, so that he could be viewed by the thousands of people who made the journey to Des Moines on purpose to see the great three-year-old stallion and race horse. About this time excitement was running high; a great many people thought that Mr. Williams was very foolish to refuse the handsome offers that had been made him for the horse. Others thought that Axtell had trotted his fastest mile, and that he was a broken down colt. But all this talk had no effect on Mr. Williams. He

had priced Axtell at $100,000, and it was begin-
ning to look as though he meant it, and just here
let us take a look at C. W. Williams as a business
man.   Time and again,  all of his marvelous success has been attributed to luck.   What   folly!
Granted  that the production of Axtell was to a
certain degree good fortune, how many  men were
there in the United States that would not have
sold Axtell when $50.000 was offered for him?
How many that would not have sold him for forty
thousand?  Yes, for twenty.  Ay, for $10,000.
How are we to account for the fact that Mr. Williams did not sell him for any of these prices?
There is but one answer.   He is a thorough business man.   He had set his  mark high on this
horse, and he was compelling everything to bend
to his iron will, pending the accomplishment of his
purpose.   Axtell made his next start at St. Louis,
Mo., October 4th, 1889.   The Horseman has it:

Exhibition mile trotting.

Axtell, b. s., by William L, C. W. Williams, 1.
     Time: 2:19.

So he has not lost all  of his speed.   True, it
is not so good as his record of 2:14.   But, remember the hardship this colt has endured.   Since the
twenty-seventh of June, he has been shipped several thousand miles, and has trotted no less than

eleven fast miles.   The average time being 2:18⅘
for the eleven miles, and a number of these he
could have trotted several seconds faster, enough
faster to have brought the average close to 2:17,
had there been any occasion for it.   As stated
above, the time had come with Axtell, when he,
or rather Mr. Williams, could make his own terms.
He is a great drawing card at race meetings, and
the management can well afford to give him a lib-
eral purse to get him on the grounds. no matter
whether he trotted to beat 2:23 or 2:14. and you
are not likely to find this man Williams driving to
beat any fast mark. unless there is something in it.
as we will soon see.

# CHAPTER VI.

### AXTELL AT TERRE HAUTE, INDIANA, MAKING HIS RECORD OF 2:12.

And now we have followed Iowa's pride for three months through changing scenes, have rejoiced when he was victorious, and been sympathetic when defeat attended him, which was seldom, then come with him to the spot where his name is made glorious, where it is to be graven upon the mind of the horse world in such brilliant letters that it will never be forgotten. We will let the Horseman tell the story:

"Terre Haute, Ind., Oct. 9, 1889. The appearance of Axtell was the signal for applause, and right royally did the enthusiastic spectators tender the famous three-year-old an ovation as he moved by the stand. He was started to go a fast mile, and was accompanied by Budd Doble's runner, Father John, with George Starr in the sulky. A mile in about 2:16 was all that was looked for, but as the first three quarters were checked off in 33 seconds, 33¾ seconds and 32¼ seconds, it looked as if Sunol's record was in danger. The last quarter, however, was not up to expectations, as it was finished in $34\frac{3}{4}$ seconds. It could have been trotted faster, as Williams did not force the youngster out as he did at Washington Park and Cleveland. Under any conditions a mile in $2:14\frac{1}{2}$ is a wonderful performance, and still more commendable when credited to a three-year-old. In this case, however, it has a strange significance, as Axtell never had harness on him for four weeks previous to his 2:19 at St. Louis, last week. Axtell has now trotted three miles below 2:15, and has more than an even chance to recover the three-year-old record, and in all probability reduce the stallion record."

Two days later Axtell makes the supreme effort of his life, and wins.

Terre Haute, Ind., October 11, 1889. Axtell's trip against the three-year-old record has proved the event of the week. It seemed impossible for him to be sucessful with so little work as he has had. When Williams appeared for a warming up mile, there was a buzz of excitement. A little later he came out for the trial, and was greeted with applause. The colt never looked so fit, but no one expected to witness the greatest mile ever trotted by a stallion. He scored twice and nodded for the word. Mr. Ijams said go, and the great colt was off for the supreme effort of his life.

Steady and true he went to the quarter in 33 seconds; he was at the half in 1:05½, the three-quarters in 1:37¼, and trotted home in exactly 2:12. As he reached the half, a silence as of death came over that audience. Some old-time and experienced horseman quietly remarked: "It is too fast." On he flew to the three-quarters, trotting straight and true as an arrow. Men looked at their watches, and the cry went up. "He will beat it, sure." Leaving the three-quarters he commenced to climb the hill. The suspense was painful. This was the crucial test, and it was generally thought that here he would fail. On he came without even a change in his pure frictionless stroke. Rounding the turn without faltering he started down the short stretch, each step bringing him nearer the championship. After having covered half the distance. Williams eased him for a breath. The crowd, wild with excitement, yelled, "come on, come on, he will beat it, sure." Responding to Williams' call, Axtell sped towards the wire like an arrow from a bow, and swept under it in 2:12, winner of the grandest heat ever trotted by a stallion, living or dead. Before he reached the wire men knew he had eclipsed all stallion records, and shouts of joy rent the air.

Williams drove a little way down the stretch, turned and came to the judge's stand, when the judges, timers and audience joined in one long, loud, exultant cry of victory, while hats went flying in the air, and ladies waved their handkerchiefs and joined in the tumultuous applause.

After the excitement had died away, Mr. Ijams, in a voice trembling with emotion, said, "Ladies and gentlemen; the wonderful colt, Axtell, has trotted a mile over this track in 2:12, the grandest mile ever trotted, and I propose three cheers for Axtell, and three more for Williams." The delighted audience responded with a will, and, amidst the plaudits of the people, Axtell was proclaimed king of stallions; king by inheritance of royal blood; king by virtue of his noble deeds.

Axtell was accompanied by Father John, driven with rare judgment by Geo. Starr. He trotted the half in 1:05¼, and the middle half in 1:04¾.

Colonel Conley, A. E. Brush and Secretary Steiner were the timers, and each watch registered exactly 2:12, while dozens of men outside made it 2:11¾. Doble, and other experts, expressed the opinion that had he two more weeks for training, he could trot a much faster mile. By this effort Axtell beats the three-year-old record a second and three-quarters, beats the stallion record a second

and one-quarter, and at one stroke wipes out all
stallion records, pacing or trotting. He is certainly the wonder of the age.

Terre Haute, Ind.. Oct. 12, 1889. Axtell's
performance is still the topic of the day, and to it
his sale for $105,000 has been added. Last eve-
ning at a dinner given by C. W. Williams, the
merits of the horse were discussed. W. P. Ijams
created a wave of applause by saying, "Mr. Williams, I am anthorized to offer you $100,000 for
Axtell."

Williams quietly replied: "l cannot accept the
offer." Mr Ijams then said: "I will give you
$5,000 for five colts from five of my best mares."
Williams declined the proposition, but said the
horse would be in service at a fee of $1,000, and
for mares which failed to stand, he would return
the money.

The party then adjourned, and as Wiliams left
the room, John Madden approached him and said:
"I want to buy your colt, Axtell, and will give
you $100,000 for him."

"I have just refused that offer," was Williams'
reply, and Madden followed it up by adding another thousand.

At this, Colonel Conley stepped up and said:
"Williams, I will give you more for Axtell than
any one; I will give you $105,000."

Williams replied; ''you can have him.''

Colonel Conley, W. P. Ijams. F. T. Moran and A. E. Brush affixed their signatures to the proper document, a check was handed Mr. Williams for a part of the amount, and the wonder of the year passed from the hands of his breeder. owner and trainer, into those of a syndicate.

At one o'clock Saturday. the colt was formally delivered to George Starr, and became a member of Budd Doble's stable.

## CHAPTER VII.

### ALLERTON AS A TWO YEAR OLD.

Allerton made his first appearance on the turf at Keokuk, Iowa, when he was two years old. He was started in a race at this place on the 8th day of August, 1888, purse $100, for two-year-olds. He was driven by John Hussey, and after losing two heats to a filly called Black Wing, he won the third, fourth and fifth heats; fastest time 2:50. The time in this race is not phenomenal, but it was good. One thing the colt showed was his ability to stay and trot. He did not attract especial attention at this time. He was good enough to win his race, and that was all that was asked of him.

He was next started at Des Moines, Iowa, at the state fair September 3rd, 1888, purse $515, for two-year-olds.

Here he is asked to trot a little faster, which he does, and wins in straight heats, time 2:49¼, 2:48½. The young fellow starts out as though he meant to win every race in which he is started. He is a good colt, was bred to trot, and no horse has a better right to do so.

His next appearance is at Independence, Iowa, Sept. 13, 1888, purse $110, for two-year-olds. He wins easily in 3:03¾, and 2:56. This is his third race, in fact, his third start, all in races, and he is winner in all of them.

At Cedar Rapids, Iowa, September 19th, he made his first start against time, 2:48½, and won in 2:43¾ Thus far he came steadily down the scale, lowering his record whenever asked to do so.

At Lexington, Kentucky, November 1st, the ambitious colt met his first defeat. Here he was started in a match against Glenview Belle, and was distanced in 2:31. The time was a little too fast, that was all.

On the same day, at the same place, he was started against time, 2:40, and again lost by one-quarter of a second. He trotted the mile in 2:40¼. Although he did not win in his last attempt, he placed 2:40¼ to his credit, a very respectable showing for a two-year-old.

Although Allerton goes into winter quarters with fewer honors than his stable companion, Axtell, still what he has done is good, and he has a great many friends, one in particular, John Hussey, the young man who has driven him and cared for him through the season.

Here we will leave him, also, to the tender mercies of C. W. Williams, and await developments.

## CHAPTER VIII.

### ALLERTON IN HIS THREE-YEAR-OLD FORM.

Allerton's first appearance on the turf in 1889, is at Cedar Rapids, Iowa, June 25, where he is entered and started in the 2:29 class, and secures third money, and this was doing remarkably well, when it is taken into consideration that he was battling against a field of aged horses, some of them with records below 2:30. He was third in 2:31¼ and second in 2:32. The Horseman says of him: "C. W. William's brown colt, Allerton, by Jay Bird, made a good showing, and satisfied the public that he is a colt that will prove himself a winner after trotting a few races."

This looks like pretty rough work on a three-year-old. But Mr. Williams evidently knows his horse, and he should be the most competent judge.

In just eight days from this time, July 3, 1889, Allerton is again started against a field of ten seasoned campaigners at Minneapolis, Minn., in the 2:37 class, for a purse of $500. He not only makes a good showing in this race, but lands first money and secures a splendid race record.

"In the 2:37 trot, ten horses made their appearance at the call. Ouida was drawn. Ichi Ban was a strong favorite, selling for $10, and the field $10. The favorite won the first heat, and then Allerton, a horse that was never thought of by the talent, went on and won the next three heats. Allerton is a three-year-old by Jay Bird, and is owned by C. W. Williams, owner of Axtell. Mr. Williams is the owner of two wonderful colts. I fully believe Allerton can beat 2:20, and I am confident he can beat any three-year-old, barring his stable companion. When the horses made their appearance for the fourth heat, Mr. Prentice, the driver of Ichi Ban, was requested by the judges to dismount, and John Splan took his seat. Splan made one of his great drives, but failed to beat the colt."

The time in this race was 2:29, 2:27, 2:26$\frac{1}{4}$, 2:24$\frac{1}{2}$. Allerton is showing himself to be a great race horse. Well, you may depend upon it that every thing that could be done, whether by fair means or otherwise, was done to defeat him. Even the judges were deceived to the extent of calling down the driver of Ichi Ban, and substituting John Splan. It would now seem that Williams' chance for winning was very poor against such a finisher as Splan was known to be, but it all made no difference. The great colt reeled off the miles just fast enough to reach the wire first and win the money.

All the trotting world was watching and waiting with interest the race at St. Paul, Minn., July 13. The day was dark and gloomy, and while many were disappointed in witnessing the race, they were *not* disappointed in the way in which Allerton acquitted himself. Six horses were entered in the race, and Allerton won in three straight heats, scoring a mark of 2:23 in the second heat, and showing that he was not merely a fair day, good weather race horse by trotting the third heat in a heavy shower in 2:24¾. Given a good track, and feeling at himself, Allerton undoubtedly, can beat 2:20 quite easily.

August 30th, at Cleveland, Ohio, Allerton is again started in a race. Although he is not victorious, he gains hosts of friends by his excellent performance. "C. W. Williams' great three-year-old colt, Allerton, drew a bad position in a field of thirteen aged starters. In the third heat he trotted around the bunch, and trotted the mile in 2:20¾. People declared it was a shame to put a three-year-old to such a test, yet an astute horse man who watched him cool out, remarked he was so little distressed and breathed so easily he would

not blow out a candle. They said it was an out-
rage, simply because it had not been done before,
forgetting it is easier for some horses to trot in
2:20 than for others to trot in 2:30. Through all
the ages the people have been unreasoning and
capricious. They declare a thing to be impossible, yet when some man or beast has accomplished a great feat they make an idol of him.
Allerton is a great colt and a race horse, and we
are breeding great colts in this day and age. The
truth is, breeding is getting to be a science, and
we progress." (Horseman.)

Quite true! Breeding *is* getting to be a science,
and it looks very much as if C. W. Williams had
mastered this particular thing. The wind-up of
the little notice in the Horseman sounds just a little as if the writer thought that there was being
too much said about Allerton or his owner, perhaps a little of both. Let us ask the question why
should Mr. Williams not receive the applause of
the nation? Who, up to this time, had done what
he had done—bred, trained and driven to their
records two colts, three years old, one with a
record of 2:14¾, the other with a record of 2:23,
and had trotted in 2:20½ in a non-winning heat in a
race? Who had done this, or come any where
near it? It is the rare things that are sought
after, and Axtell's, Allerton's and C. W. Williams'

are most certainly in this class. If there is a nation on the face of the earth that has anything in this line that will compare with this trio, we would like to see it.

Three days later. August 2nd. Mr. Williams started Allerton against time 2:23, winning in 2:20¼. The next day, August 3rd, he is again started against 2:20½, winning in 2:19. Although he did not win the race at Cleveland, he has reduced his record twice, gaining a mark of 2:19. Good enough!

Allerton is shipped from Cleveland to Chicago, to attend the Northwestern Breeders' meeting, and take a hand in the races. The first race in which he participates is the 2:35 class; purse $2,000. The Horseman describes it thus: "Today the question in the 2:35 stake is, can the great three-year-old Allerton beat a good field of aged horses? It is the opinion of the most astute horsemen that he can, and they are, before the first heat, freely exchanging the "Lincoln green" for bits of paste board on which is written Allerton, $50, field $50. Victoria Wilkes was installed as second choice, and many friends of the Onwards and Dictators were firm in the belief that she would lead the colt a merry dance.

The first heat was called, and as the word was given, the bay stallion, Poem, by General Wash-

ington, assumed the lead and held it to the distance. Allerton was a fair second to the head of
the stretch, and Victoria Wilkes third. From this
point Williams began to drive, and foot by foot
gained on Poem, sending him to a series of breaks
and beating him at the wire in 2:21¼.

The second heat was called, and Allerton sold
for $50, and the field $15. Allerton took the lead
and was never headed. Poem kept at his wheel,
frequently indulging in his handy breaks, for
which he was set back to third place. Victoria
Wilkes made a spurt on the upper turn, and looked
like a contestant, but died away in the stretch and
got sixth place.

The third heat was a surprise. There was no
betting, the race being conceded to Allerton. The
word was given, and at once Allerton broke and
could not settle to a trot until the entire field had
passed him. John W. led to the head of the
stretch, where Victoria Wilkes assumed the lead
and won at will in 2:25½, Alric was second, Poem
third and John W. fourth.

The fourth heat was considered a sure thing
for Allerton. The result showed that even the
wise men sometimes have to "guess again," as it
was won in 2:25½ by John W., with Victoria
Wilkes second, and Alric third. The fifth heat
was intensely exciting. Alric took the lead and

maintained it to the three quarters, where Allerton came to his wheel. There was a pretty race down the stretch between Allerton, John W. and Alric. Allerton won, John W. was second, and Alric third, in 2:24. Allerton is a sure enough race horse."

August 23, 1889, still finds Allerton at Chicago, where he is entered in the 2:27 class; purse, $2,000. "The first regular race on the day's program was the Washington Park stake, for the 2:27 class. The starters were So Long, Silver Cloud, Elista, Bassenger Boy, Erin, Dixie V., Allerton, Alaric and Glamour. In the betting. Allerton sold for $25, Elista $20, Bassenger Boy $13, Alaric $5, and the field $15. Silver Cloud drew the pole. On the third score the word was given, with Bassenger Boy on a break. Allerton went to the front and was never headed. Silver Cloud was second all the way, Dixie V. third and Elista fourth, until near the wire, when Starr called on her for a brush, and she finished third.

Before the second heat Bassenger Boy sold for $25, Allerton $20, Elista $15, field $8. Allerton simply marched off and won the heat in 2:21. Elista was second to the upper turn, where Bassenger Boy took second place and made play for the heat. At the distance he had crept to Aller-

5

ton's girth and the crowd shouted: "Bassenger wins," but Williams let go the colt's head, and it was all over.

The race was now conceded to Allerton, and when the word was given the Jay Bird colt pulled away from the field and trotted one of the fastest heats on record, and had it been made yesterday before Faust secured his 2:18, it would have been the fastest for a three-year-old in a race. Bassenger Boy kept the colt company to the head of the stretch, the first three quarters being finished in $35\frac{1}{4}$, 35 and $34\frac{2}{4}$ seconds. Turning into the stretch Williams made his drive, sending Allerton the last quarter in $33\frac{1}{4}$ seconds, making the mile in $2:18\frac{1}{4}$. The applause at the finish was almost deafening."

Two great victories in the compass of four days! Two thousand dollars in cool cash aside from the increased value of the horse! Remember, Allerton is but three years old; he is a stallion with his whole life before him. It would not be strange if Mr. Williams were to become a little vain after gaining so many victories, and rising in one short year from the ordinary walks of life to a position where his name is fast becoming famous throughout the land. But not so. He is the same matter of fact, hard working man that he has always been.

Allerton's next performance is at Independence, Iowa, against time 2:23, for a purse of $500. Allerton wins easily in 2:22.

He makes his next start at Des Moines, Iowa, September 3. 1889; stake for foals of 1886. After winning two heats, Allerton went lame and was drawn. This proved to be a serious matter. He was left at Des Moines in charge of John Hussey, and it was three weeks before he could be moved, and at the end of that time, it required an hour to lead him one half mile. This ended his work for the season. In fact it was thought that he had trotted his last mile. But good care brought him through the winter, and early in the spring he was able to jog, although still quite lame. Had his owner been a man of less determination, there might have been lost to the turf the grandest race horse that ever scored for the word.

# CHAPTER IX.

### ALLERTON AS A FOUR YEAR OLD.

Allerton's first public performance as a four-year-old is at Independence, Iowa, on the new kite shaped track, at the first meeting held on the new grounds at Rush Park. The Horseman, dated July 17, 1890, speaks of it as follows:

"While the horses were getting ready for the 2:45 trot, Allerton was brought out to warm up for a mile. His appearance on the track was acknowledged by deafening shouts by the spectators. Although he showed signs of lameness, he went with that determination characteristic of a great race horse. After a little jogging, he was driven a mile to beat 2:18¼. The first heat he knocked off one-quarter of a second. Mr. Williams not being satisfied with that mark, he was driven three heats more, obtaining a record of 2:16¾ in the third heat."

Although the great colt has been lame, and it has been prophesied that he would never again trot a fast mile, he has already trotted the fastest heat of the year, in a record-breaking mile.

His next start is at Detroit, Michigan, in the Horseman's Great Expectation Stake. This event is well written up by the correspondent of Clark's Horse Review:

"Detroit, Michigan, July 24, 1890. The Great Expectation stake was called. It was a stake opened four years ago by The Horseman, and was extremely valuable. There were five starters; Baroness, by Mambrino, dam by Mambrino Patchen; Navidad, by Whips; Margaret S., by Director; Allerton, by Jay Bird; and Sir Walter Scott, by North Star. It was conceded by all horsemen that the contest for first place was narrowed down to the great stallion, Allerton, and the superb filly, Margaret S: They alternated as favorites, according to the disposition of the crowd. Allerton had trotted on July 4th to a record of 2:16¾, and Margaret S. had won a third heat at Saginaw, in 2:17½. The word was given to an excellent start, and Margaret S. shot to the front, and at the quarter was lengths in the lead. Allerton broke on the turn and was way out; McDowell drove Margaret S. right along to the half in 1:08¼, and at this point it looked as though the others were distanced. At the head of the stretch, he set out to drive in dead earnest, and swept under the wire in 2:18¼, with all the others outside the flag except Allerton, who was, according to the distance judge, inside by a neck. The heat aroused intense excitement, and the general belief was that Margaret S. had distanced the entire field. It was such a surprise that the vast audience had litttle to say, and anxiously awaited the vedict. The judges deliberated some time and rigidly examined the distance judge, who was firm in his declaration that Allerton was in. When Mr. Campan arose to announce the decision, there were few in the audience who expected to hear that there would be another heat in the great stake. Margaret S. was first and Allerton second. It was dark and cloudy when the second heat was called. Margaret S. at once set the pace, and at the half was two lengths in the lead. From this point Allerton began to creep up. and one of the grandest finishes ever seen on a race track ensued. The superb pair trotted steadily and very fast. each with true, regular stroke, neither making a skip or bobble. The filly maintained a decided advantage until well inside the distance, when Allerton got to her girth, and creeping up inch by inch. finally swept under the wire winner, by half a length, of one of the grandest heats ever trotted. The time was 2:16¼, and the last half was trotted in 1:06½, and the track was estimated to be two seconds slow. The immense audience was excited to frenzied enthusiasm at the great finish, and Wil-'

liams, with the grand colt, was received with tremendous applause. It was a heat, the like of which is rarely seen. The last heat had scarcely been trotted when a terrible storm arose. The lightning flashed, the thunder roared, and the flood gates of heaven were opened and the rain descended in torrents upon the just and the unjust, and in two minutes the track was transformed into a sea of sticky mud. The races were therefore postponed until next day.

On Friday morning the sun came out, and at one o'clock the track was in moderately good condition. The free-for all pace was first on the card, and Adonis won it without a struggle in 2:20¼, and 2:18¾; Grey Harry, second.

Next there was the great contest between the four-year-olds, Allerton and Margaret S. Concerning the question as to whether Allerton was outside the flag in the first heat, there were "many men of many minds." Each and every man was positive he was right. However, there was but one course for the judges, and that was to accept the distance judge's declaration. So Allerton was in it, and sold in the pools at fifty to sixteen dollars for the mare. Just why any one should think there were such odds that any lame horse could beat Margaret the writer failed to understand. The first heat was called and Margaret, as heretofore, shot out and placed herself two or three lengths in the lead at the half. Here Williams made his drive, with Allerton, and entering the stretch, was only a short distance behind. McDowell made the mistake of selecting the pole which was heavy and muddy, and Williams swung to the right, where the footing was good. The result was the filly tired in the mud, and Allerton won the heat by a neck in 2:18¼. Then it rained again and the track got worse. The next heat McDowell adopted different tactics, and allowed the filly to brush for a lead, which she got at once, but took her back and saved a brush for the finish. Entering the stretch he chose the outside, and the race down the stretch was grand. Three lengths from the wire it looked Allerton's heat, but Andy let go the filly's head and she won with a great burst of speed, by a neck, in 2:23¼. The next heat was to decide a big stake. Margaret at once took a lead and, before reaching the quarter, Allerton broke and broke badly. He danced up and down and would not trot. When Margaret was at the half it was a foregone conclusion that she could distance the colt, and McDowell drove right along, winning at ease in 2:20¾. Allerton was hopelessly distanced. Margaret won the entire stakes, amounting to $9,450. The colt and filly were each bred by their present owners, and by them entered in the stake. When Allerton won the second heat in 2:16¼, Williams remarked that it was no disgrace to the filly to be beaten in that time by a colt like Allerton. That was true, and it was no disgrace to Allerton to be beaten by a filly like Margaret."

Another great race decided, and although our hero did not win, he has again demonstrated the fact that he is the greatest race stallion on earth.

Allerton is next started in the 2:16 class at Terre Haute, Indiana, October 10th, 1890, for a purse of $1,000. Here he trots a good race, and wins in straight heats; time 2:20, 2:17½ and 2:15½. He has not lost any of his racing qualities since his great struggle at Detroit. Three heats, the average time of which is 2:17⅔, is something wonderful when it is taken into consideration that Allerton was still suffering from lameness. The question was often asked, what would he do if he was good on all of his legs?

The next engagement is at Lexington, Kentucky, October 14th, in the 2:19 class, for a purse of $5,000. Here the courageous colt is to meet the mighty McDoel and his illustrious driver, Budd Doble, the pair that have won during the season twenty-one heats in an average time of a little better than 2:20. The race is described in Clark's Horse Review as follows:

"The great race of the meeting was the 2:19 stake for $5,000. The starters were McDoel, Allerton, Hendryx, Stevie, Keno F, Walter E, Diamond and Henrietta. It was a grand race, and its prominent features can be expressed in a few words. The contest for first money narrowed down to the speedy McDoel and the wonderful four-year-old, Allerton. Stevie had to trot the best race of his life to carry off third money. Almost all interest centered in the contest for first money. All the other horses were good, and except for the quality of these two, would have been noticeable factors. The whole point was in a nut shell. It was known that McDoel could trot a mile in 2:15 or better, and could brush a quarter in 31 seconds. All that ought to beat almost any horse; but was he game when pinched and carried two or three miles to his clip? That no one knew, for he had not been tested. It was known that Allerton was capable of a mile in about 2:15, and when in condition would stay all day, and in any event was one of the grandest horses that ever looked through a bridle. He had only been four weeks out of paddock, and it seemed outside the bounds of reason that any horse thus short of condition for a punishing race could stay and beat McDoel. These were the conditions that influenced the betting, and McDoel sold favorite, but

Allerton was well up. As the horses appeared on the track there was a little ripple of excitement, for people felt they were to see a battle of giants fought to the death. The first heat McDoel won with all ease, with Hendryx second, Stevie third and Allerton fourth. It was an easy heat in 2:19¼. The second heat McDoel won, but Allerton was after him from the half, and finished a close second, with Walter E third. It was in 2:17½, and neither Allerton nor McDoel had been extended. But now they were together, side by side, and people knew the next heat would be war to the knife. As they scored for the third heat the excitement was intense. Four or five times they scored amid a silence as of death. Then there went up through the great concourse of men and women that mesmeric feeling that is sometimes created by a repressed excitement, as they turned the last time and came head and head for the word. All barriers were swept away, all restraint thrown off and with one accord, men and women arose to their feet and stood on benches and wherever there was foothold, feeling that the time had come and the great battle would commence. The word was given and with a rush they went around the turn, and on they flew to the stretch. With an electrical burst of speed Allerton rushed to the front, and Doble let him go, content to lay in his wheel.

Full well he knew the only way to beat the greatest
racer of his age that e'er the sun shone on was to
wait, and at the last call for all the reserve of Mc-
Doel's .wonderful brush.    So they went to the half
in 1:07½, and to the three-quarter in 1:42½.    The
tactics were the same.    As they swung into the
stretch excitement was at fever heat.    The time
was fast and now was the critical moment.    Could
the colt stand that fearful brush down the stretch?
All who knew him knew he would fight till he
died, but did he have the speed?    Heading into
the stretch, just on the crest of the hill.    Doble,
with all his matchless skill, commenced his drive.
Down that hill they came like a cyclone, that in
its mad career would sweep everything before it
off' the earth.    On they come, and now McDoel
begins to gain.    The colt trots just as fast, but
that gelding's almost superhuman flight of speed
began to tell.    He was at the stallion's girth, then
inch by inch he gained until his head was reached.
Then Doble gathered him together, and asked
him for one do or die effort.    Nobly he responded
and on he came, gaining foot by foot.    He was
clearly in the lead.    At the distance Allerton
broke, and through that great audience there could
be heard a sigh, like the sobbing of the wind
among the pines, for their hearts were with the
great youngster who, single handed and alone, was

gamely fighting one of the giants of the turf. But see! He's caught again! It was only a little break, for tired, exhausted nature demanded some relief. Yes, he's caught again, and Williams gently applied the whip. Heavens! what a change! All the pride of his noble nature resented the indignity; every drop of royal blood that pulsated from his great heart warmed at the insult, and with head high in air, with his great nostrils widely expanded and his beautiful eyes flashing fire, he rallied for one last grand, almost despairing effort, and on he came, looking in his wrath and sublime determination for all the world like a demon incarnate, and fifty yards from the wire, with unfaltering stride, he had McDoel's wheel, and step by step he gained until he swept under the wire, winner by a length of one of the grandest heats ever trotted on all the earth. McDoel had made his marvelous brush. It was all over, and Allerton for the second time had trotted a third heat in 2:15$\frac{1}{2}$. Dear reader, were you ever in a storm at sea? Have you heard the terrific roar of the angry waves as they dashed, mountains high, against your ill fated craft? Do you remember the intense calm and silence that preceded the storm? Well, for a moment just such a silence, and then, as the grandeur of the heat became understood, there arose from that audience a mighty shout,

a yell of joy and gladness that rose and fell and
rose again till it waked the echoes through all the
region of the blue grass. Men shouted and shook
hands, and then all yelled again. Women stood
on the seats and laughed and cheered and cheered
and laughed. It was a great battle worthily won
by one of the grandest horses ever born unto the
earth. When it was time for the horses to go
again it was too dark, and 'postponed until to-
morrow' was announced.

The fourth heat was nearly the same as the one
the night before, except that Allerton could not
win, but trotted in 2:16 and forced McDoel to trot
in 2:15½."

It would be useless to try to add anything to
this eloquent rehearsal of the great race, suffice it
to say that it was truly wonderful.

After the Lexington meeting Allerton is not
started again until the fall meeting at Independence.
A short account of this meeting will give the
reader some idea of the rapid strides Independence was making as a great horse center, and the
kite-shaped track at Rush Park, in particular, was
already famous throughout the horse world.

It looked like folly to undertake a meeting so
late in the season, but people are beginning to
have faith in the so-called "Lucky Williams."

The public are learning to know that he is an excellent business man, that there is method in all that he does, and that they can depend upon him.

Late in the season as it is, we find a large number of entries. There is something near two hundred and fifty entries in class races, and a host of candidates for standard stakes. There were nineteen class races, the purse the same in each, $300; the purses being the same in the trotting and pacing classes.

At first glance we are surprised that so many horses would enter in these races so late in the season, but after more mature deliberation the reason is very plain. The Independence mile track is the fastest on earth, and breeders desirous of obtaining records flocked there in great numbers from the Atlantic to the Pacific.

Independence is a world-famed little city already. No need now, when speaking of Independence, to add Iowa; every one knows what is meant. The name of Allerton and Independence have become inseparably connected, never to be separated. In ages to come, gray-haired grandfathers will relate to bright-eyed boys the story of Allerton, Axtell and C. W. Williams.

At this meeting Allerton was again started against his record, on October 23d, 1890. He was started against time 2:15½ and trotted in 2:14, reducing his own record and clipping a second off of the four-year-old stallion record.

On October 28th, he was again started against 2:14, making two trials and trotting both miles in exactly 2:15. He failed to reduce his record, but trotted two wonderful miles.

October 30th, he is again sent to beat 2:14, but failed, trotting in 2:28 and 2:14, equalling but not lowering his record.

November 1st, he is again speeded on the enchanted course, this time a winner; Allerton against time 2:14; won, time 2:13¾. Again, the same day, he goes against 2:13¾, and clips off one-quarter of a second, giving him a mark of 2:13½.

This ends, for the season of 1890, the turf career of the grandest four-year-old that the world has ever seen. He has won more heats inside of 2:30 than any other horse of his age ever did. In his three and four-year-old form he has placed thirty-four heats to his credit. Nancy Hanks, 2:14½, won twenty-nine heats inside of 2:30, although she has not trotted anything like the number of fast heats in races that Allerton has, as she has in all cases out-classed her competitors, and every heat trotted, with a single exception, has been credited to her, while Allerton has been in the hottest company and lost many fast heats.

# CHAPTER X.

ALLERTON REDUCING HIS RECORD AS A FVE-YEAR-OLD. HIS GREAT RACE WITH NANCY HANKS AND MARGARET S.

Allerton, in the spring of 1891, was perhaps in better form than he had ever been. He had been jogged ten to fifteen miles per day through the winter when the weather would admit, and the first time that he was started he gave evidence that he still retained his speed. As early as the middle of April he trotted an eighth in $17\frac{1}{2}$ seconds and had already been bred to thirty-two mares. He was given an abundance of work through the stud season, more than most trainers would have recommended under the circumstances. About the first week in June he was given his first mile in 2:27, moving along at a lively clip in the last half.

He continued to show good form, and at the July meeting at Independence was started against his record of $2:13\frac{1}{2}$, from which he clips one-half second, and did it in grand style. This is a won-

6

derful performance when it is remembered that he is still in the stud, having had sixty-nine mares to his embrace during the season.

In a few days after lowering his record to 2:13, he trotted a quarter in 31¼ seconds. The great son of Jay Bird was being watched with a great deal of interest at this time, for, be it remembered, he was entered in the great five-year-old race to be trotted over the Independence course in August. It was the opinion of a majority of the horsemen throughout the country that he would not be fit after a heavy season in the stud. However, he continued to improve, and on the 5th day of August clipped another second off his record, trotting the mile without a skip in 2:12!

At last the great feat is accomplished! Is there anything significant about this record? A little less than two years ago C. W. Williams drove the great three-year-old, Axtell, in exactly the same time. What other man has done such a thing— the first colts ever foaled his, and he has driven them both to this amazingly low record. Ah! there is something beside good luck in all this. There is good management, good judgment, and a world of perseverance.

After this performance, the great stallion and race horse is simply kept in the best possible condition, the long looked for race being near at hand.

The event is so ably described in the Horseman that we will give it to our readers as we find it in the issue of September 3d, 1891:

"Thursday dawned bright and cool and clear at Independence. At last the great day had arrived, and from the four points of the compass, afoot, on horseback, in 'lumber' wagons, freight cars and Pullmans, thousands streamed across the prairie to witness the widely heralded duel between Nancy Hanks and Allerton. Long before noon the meagre seating capacity of Rush Park's grand stand was overtaxed. At 1 o'clock the lawn and quarter stretch were densely packed, the infield crowded a full furlong from the start and finish, while along the picket fences, upon grand stand roofs, and stable roofs men stood or clung wherever a glimpse of the course might be had. And when at 2 o'clock Williams, with flushed face, moved Allerton down the stretch cheers rose and hands were clapped in admiration by more than 20,000 spectators. The stallion was truly grand. A bit of blue was twined in the braided foretop, and his rich mahogany coat flashed back the rays of sunlight as he jogged along, ears pricked, inquisitively surveying the surging crowd. Power united with resolution was the impression his appearance conveyed. Allerton has filled and grown in muscular development within the year last past.

To-day he is the picture of a powerful trotting race horse. At no point in his make-up is there a shade of the grossness so often mistaken for substance, yet from the enormously deep shoulder and brisket back to the broad, swelling stifles one sees an embodiment of power which is almost awe-inspiring. The five-year-old is something lacking in length and range, however. He is not racy-looking or really handsome. But he is grand to the fullest sense of the term.

Williams brought him to the post in almost perfect condition. If Doble had been working on Nancy Hanks the season through with a single eye to shaping her for this event, the Independence man had done but little less, although of course his horse was at a great disadvantage, having made a stud season of seventy-six mares, extending up to within a very few weeks of the race. Williams, however, had managed to keep the stallion hard and strong by roading him fifteen miles a day all through the preceding winter and early spring, until the track grew fit for fast work, when active preparation for the race was begun, right in the height of the breeding season. In his warming up work he sweated out clear and free, showing he was not far from right. If Allerton suggests power, his great rival typified speed. Nancy Hanks' fine, blood-like neck, high

croup, deep, drooping quarters and Sunol-like con-
formation make her almost a model, except in
point of size, of what the queen of the turf should
be. The little bay mare never before looked so
eager, so fit, or so full of speed as when Doble
breezed her through the stretch in her preliminary
work. She was even rank and almost unruly,
such was her anxiety to go. As for the other
starter, Margaret S, the great filly that had trotted the Independence track in 2:12¼, as a four-
year-old, her coat was dull, she had a baked-up
look, and could not begin to speed like the Kentucky mare. A delegation of Kentuckians and
southerners such as one seldom sees on a Northern
race track were on hand to witness the race, and
they poured money into the pool-box on the Happy
Medium Mare. Heavy betting had been going on
since the beginning of the week. At first the
odds were two to one on Nancy against the horse.
But the night before, at the down-town pool-room,
when Lowry called for bids on the big race of the
week, and John Madden, resting his elbows on the
railing of the stand and assuming an attitude of
determination, bid $500 for choice, taking Hanks,
only $235 could be had for the Allerton end, even
though the genteel auctioneer pleaded well for the
chance of the stallion, arguing, after the opinion
held by many, that although the filly might be the

faster of the two, her Happy Medium blood would come to the surface when she was called upon to go three heats right close to the limit of her speed, and the dead-game son of Jay Bird would beat her to the end.   After this the odds on the mare grew longer, until just before the start it was $100 to $40, Nancy against the field.   Nearly all the shrewdest turfmen  seemed to think the filly must win.   They relied almost wholly upon her supposed superior speed.   It was generally conceded that in case Allerton should prove her equal or near it in this respect, his matchless gameness and capacity to repeat would give the victory to him. But the mare was fully two seconds faster, a good many were inclined to believe.   She had trotted the  tracks at Rochester and  Chicago in 2:12¼, while Allerton had bettered this time but a quarter of a second over the much faster track at Independence.   Doble himself had been heard to say when Nelson trotted in 2:10¾ the day before that he  would  match  the five-year-old in his stable against the stallion king for either a dash, a repeat or a race of heats, three in five.   This was equivalent to saying Nancy Hanks could, if called upon, trot better than 2:11.   Before the three contestants had scored more than once or twice, an incident occurred which went very far to confirm the belief that Nancy had the speed of Allerton, with a good deal besides to spare. Doble turned well back of the other two, up above the crossing, and fifty yards from the wire the stallion, coming on at top speed, must have been fully two lengths ahead of the little mare. But from there she came with such an astonishing rush that before the stand was reached Allerton's advantage was but the length of his neck, and Nancy seemed to be going right through the other two. This display of speed opened the eyes of a good many people, and it is said that some Allerton men sought the hedge without waiting to see anything more. On the fourth attempt they got away to a very even start, Allerton at the pole. It was Williams' plan to make the pace hot from the very start, hoping to carry the mare so fast to the half with the dead-game stallion he drove that she would wilt in the home stretch, or failing in this, to make her go the full mile at a cracking rate, which would leave her unable to repeat and come back three heats below the limit of Allerton's speed. He therefore let the brown horse sail as soon as the word was given, covering the first quarter in 0:32½ —a 2:10 gait—and then increasing the pace to a 2:06 gait in the next, Doble's rapid-gaited race mare the while not more than a head to the rear, and actually seeming to be going within herself, while Allerton was clearly enough strung out to

his utmost reach.  Beyond the half in 1:04 the
killing clip was maintained, and then it was seen
that the heat, at least, and probably the race, be-
longed to Nancy Hanks, for her bay muzzle, head
and neck appeared in front as she drew away
slightly, until rounding into the stretch her lead
was a full open length.  Doble might have taken
the pole if he had chosen to do so, and thereby
forced Williams to pull out and go around in making his drive, but instead, as if he himself was
anxious not to take any advantage whatever, Budd
left him the track for his finish.  Allerton had
little need of it, however.  He had gone his limit
all the way, while the mare was coming on ap-
parently at ease, her driver glancing over his
shoulder once or twice to see where Allerton was.
Near the distance Williams called on his horse for
a hopeless final effort.  The great colt rallied,
pumped out though he was, and tried to make a
finish worthy of himself.  Trotting too fast he
went to a break, falling back a couple of lengths,
then catching quickly came on with such a rush
that at the wire he was again on Nancy's wheel.
A storm of cheers followed the close finish—close
because Doble had not made a visible move to drive
his mare—and when Starter Walker announced
the winner's time, 2:12, a second faster than the
previous race record, applause burst forth again.

If Williams had rated Allerton with a view to driving him in the fastest possible time, instead of setting the pace so hot at the start in the hope of killing the mare, it is not at all unlikely Hanks would have had to go in 2:11 or better to win, but she could have done it without any manner of doubt. It was clear enough after this exhibition that Nancy Hanks had the speed to win. Unless she should prove unable to repeat, her victory was assured. The young mare had gone the mile well within herself; she was out of a Dictator dam—a line as stout as any thoroughbred strain in the stud-book—and there was no reason to believe she would wilt. Although Allerton came back in savage style, forcing her to trot the second heat in 2:12¾ and the third in 2:12 again, she was easily equal to the task, Doble never having to make a move in order to land his filly a winner. Williams stuck to his original plan in each of the following heats, carrying Nancy Hanks to the half as fast as Allerton could go, once in 1:05 and then in 1:05½, hoping the Happy Medium mare might crack at the last under the trying test. But for the stallion's double break in the second mile, when he rushed away too fast, the time of every heat of the race would have been as fast as 2:12. As it was, the winner beat the race record in three consecutive heats, while Allerton's time at the wire was 2:12¼, 2:13½ and 2:13, a performance which no other stallion in the world has ever equaled or even approached. Notwithstanding the fact that he was defeated, the Jay Bird colt came out of the fray more popular with turfmen than he had been before. Nancy Hanks was too fast for him. That was all. It is no sure thing that Doble could not have driven his filly the opening heat below the five-year-old record, 2:10¾, of Jay-Eye-See. She looks to be that good."

The correspondent to the Horseman says that the great Jay Bird colt made hosts of friends by his wonderful performance. Well deserved praise! What other horse is there above ground that can anywhere near equal it? To use a turf expression, he trotted the three miles "on his toes."

# CHAPTER XI.

### ALLERTON, THE KING OF TROTTING STALLIONS—2:09¼

Although Allerton was defeated in the great race with Nancy Hanks, he is not done yet. That was simply a keying-up performance. On August 31, just four days later, he is started against his record of 2:12, trotting the mile without a break in 2:11, clipping another second from his already low record.

His shoes in front had been changed since his race, for a pair weighing five ounces each, while those behind weighed only three.

On September 4th, he is again started. In a supplement to the American Trotter, dated September 3, 1891, is the following:

"The sun was just sinking into the west, when the cheers of the audience announced the coming of the king of stallions. Allerton shook his head and pranced. as if he was a colt fresh from the pasture. instead of one who had within nine short days gone the fastest race of the century. and then four days after trotted a mile only equalled

by two stallions since trotting began. He was
rank and wanted to be given his head, and it took
the combined efforts of two grooms to hold him,
till his driver could climb into the sulky.

He scored by the stand a couple of times, and
then got the word, going like a steam engine.
Hussey went after him with the runner, and he
reached the quarter, going as true as a piece of
machinery, in exactly $32\frac{1}{4}$ seconds. Williams
took him back around the turn, passing the half
under a strong pull, in $1:05\frac{1}{2}$. From there to the
three-quarter pole he gathered speed with every
stroke, and the third stage of his record breaking
trip was made in 1:38.

Here John Hussey brought up the runner,
and Allerton shook his head with that peculiar
determined gesture so often noted when he begins
one of his irresistible rushes, and finished the
mile at close to a two-minute gait, stopping the
watches at two minutes and ten seconds. Only
once did Williams call on him, and then it was
inside the distance, and he came away as if he
was just at the start, instead of the finish, of a
supreme effort.

The crowd went wild, and long continued
cheering conveyed to the people in the city, a
mile away, the intimation that something unusual
had happened.

Cheers were proposed and given with a will, for Williams, the fastest stallion on earth, the kite shaped track, and finally for John Hussey and Old Ned Gordon, the faithful runner, that has rated most of the record-breaking miles in the last ten years. Mr. Williams has just cause to be the proudest man on earth. He has, by every test, the greatest stallion on earth, not lacking in a single point.

The time announced was that of the slowest watch in the stand. Many prominent horsemen, among them, Mr. Salisbury, made the time 2:09¾, and so did one of the official timers."

A few days after, he again trotted in 2:10, and had he not made a break when almost to the wire, would have again lowered his record. Again, in less than one week, he marched off a mile in 2:10½.

Nine days later, September 19th, he is again started to beat his record of 2:10, which had been equalled the day before by Nelson. He went the first quarter in 32¾ seconds, the half in 1:05½, to the three quarters in 1:37½, and the mile in 2:09¼.

The crowd went wild with enthusiasm. Of all the watches held on this mile, not one registered slower than 2:09¼, and by far the greatest number caught the time in 2:08¾. It is believed by prominent horsemen, that had Allerton received his just dues, he would stand to-day on an equal foot-

ing in point of record with Palo Alto, 2:08¾.
After a rest of one day, this veritable bull dog
again reels off a mile in 2:09¼. He certainly is
not a quitter.

Again, September 25th, he is started against
his record of 2:09¼. He failed to lower it, but
came within one quarter of a second of it, trotting
the mile in 2:09½.

On the same afternoon, after a rest of one hour,
he is started against the world's wagon record
of 2:20, for stallions, made in 1890, over the
Independence track, by Delmarch. It was the
second time that Allerton had ever been hitched
to a wagon. However, he goes away, trotting the
mile in a strong, determined manner, in 2:15.

About this time the public were clamorous
for a meeting between our hero, the great eastern
stallion, Nelson, 2:10, and Nancy Hanks, 2:09.
Indeed, some of our Yankee neighbors had gone
so far as to insinuate that the kite-shaped track at
Independence was not a full mile. But this
question was quickly settled by the sworn statement of the county surveyor of Buchanan County,
which proved the track to be one foot and two
inches over a mile. Again exception was taken,
and it was said that the watches which were held
on Allerton were slow in starting and quick to
stop. Mr. Nelson, when giving the time of his

horse, proudly added, "regulation," after the 2:10,
meaning that his horse had obtained his record
over a regulation track.

Mr. Williams offered every inducement to per-
suade these men to come to Independence, but all
to no purpose. He hesitated to ship so valuable
a horse as Allerton, having been offered only a
short time previous, $200,000 for him. How-
ever, it seemed the only way out of it, was to go
and trot; arrangements were made to meet Nelson
at Grand Rapids, Michigan, October 8th, for a
purse of $10,000, all to go to the winner, and no
entrance fee; also, to meet Nancy Hanks at Lexington, Kentucky, October 15th, for a purse of
$8,000, the conditions being the same. The
Grand Rapids race is ably described in the Ameri
can Trotter, dated October 15, 1891.

# CHAPTER XII.

### THE ALLERTON—NELSON RACE.

GRAND RAPIDS, MICH., Oct. 8, 1891.

"This place, to-day, was the cynosure upon which the eyes of all the trotting world was turned, for here a contest for supremacy between two stallions, each claiming the title of King, was decided. Never before in the history of the trotting turf had an animal with a record as fast as 2:10 ever started in a race, but to-day two entire horses, one with a record of 2:09¼, the other with a mark of 2:10, were engaged to settle, once for all, the disputed point, as to which was entitled to the first honor. Allerton's mark of 2:09¼ had been made over the kite-shaped track at Independence. Nelson's mark of 2:10, secured over the regulation course at this place, was claimed by his friends to be the most creditable performance of the two. The conditions of the contest were such that the advantage lay with the Maine horse. He was started this season over the various fast courses of the country, and the track on which he made his fastest mile was the one selected for the battle royal. On the other hand, Allerton had received all his training on the kite-shaped track, and the only fast work he had received this season on any other course, was the mile in 2:21½, given him here last Monday.

This afternoon Allerton was given a few miles of easy exercise and then newly shod, with seven and one-half ounce shoes forward, and five ounce shoes behind. Nelson was not seen upon the track in the morning, but his owner, seated upon a box in front of his horse's stall, said that ·he never entered a race with as tranquil a feeling as he did this one.· and appeared confident of success. The track at this place is fair for a new one; it is built of clay loam, but, unless constantly kept wet and worked, is inclined to be mealy and cuppy; the turns are also too flat. As early as nine o'clock this morning, the people began to flock to the well appointed grounds of the West Michigan Fair Association. and by one o'clock, the elegant grand stand, seated with chairs, and another built for the occasion, capable of seating over 5.000 people, were filled to their utmost capacity. The infield was crowded and the outside fence was lined for half a mile with eager spectators. At least 20,000 people had assembled to witness the

coming contest. At one o'clock, Nelson, driven
by his groom, jogged by the stand, and was greeted by rounds of applause. After being driven
two miles the reverse way of the track, Mr. Nelson mounted the sulky, and as he did so, the
cheers were deafening. Mr. Nelson bowed his
acknowledgment. About five minutes later,
Allerton, driven by his owner, appeared and received generous applause, which Mr. Williams acknowledged by lifting his cap. It was evident
that the sympathies of the majority were with the
Maine representative, as was but natural, after
witnessing his previous performance here. Both
stallions were in the pink of condition. Nelson
looked fit for the race of his life, and the handsome son of Jay Bird acted as though he knew
that the honor of the mighty house he represent-
ed depended upon his efforts. After being warmed up the stallions were taken to the barn to be
cooled out and made ready for the coming race.
that was being discussed from the Atlantic to the
Pacific, and the news of which was anxiously
awaited at every telegraph office in the land. At
1:30. Mr. Leathers rang the bell of the judge's
stand and addressed the multitude, as follows:
·Ladies and gentlemen. you have assembled here
to-day to witness what I believe will be the greatest contest ever seen. The two trotting kings

meet here to-day, to do battle for the highest honors, Allerton, owned by C. W. Williams. of Independence, Iowa, with a record of 2:09¼, and
Nelson, owned by C. H. Nelson, of Waterville,
Maine, with a record of 2:10. Both are wonderful stallions, and their performance to-day will oc-
cupy a brilliant page in turf history. The purse
is $10,000, all of which goes to the winner. The
loser, however, will receive $500 for expenses.
The horses are driven by their respective breeders
and owners. In addition to the stallion race,
there will be a 2:17 trotting class, for a purse of
$1,000. President D. J. Campau, of the Detroit
Association, will officiate as starting judge, the
other judges being S. A. Browne, of Kalamazoo,
C. L. Benjamin, of Saginaw, and L. C. Webb, of
Macon. The timers are R. A. Munger, of Detroit, Thos. McAloon. of Bangor, Maine. and B.
W. Tabor, of Independence, Iowa.' After the
announcement, which was received with cheers,
the first heat of the 2:17 trot was made. and then
the track was smoothed for the champions. In
the pools the prevailing odds were, Allerton $25,
and Nelson $20. Last night some pools were sold
at Allerton $120 to Nelson $100, and a few at $50
even money. At the close of last night's sale.
however, Allerton sold for $100 to $66 for Nelson. At two o'clock. Williams and Nelson weigh

in. and Mr. Campau, tapping the bell for silence,
said:    'The rules of the Association of which
this Society is a member, require that when drivers are twenty pounds over weight, that it shall
be announced.    We find that Mr. Nelson weighs
170 pounds, twenty pounds overweight, and Mr.
Williams, 165 pounds, fifteen pounds overweight.'
This announcement was somewhat of a surprise
when some had been led to believe that Mr. Nelson weighed thirty pounds overweight.    While
waiting for their horses to appear. the owners
chatted pleasantly together in front of the judge's
stand, the brilliant colors of the driver of the
Maine horse in striking contrast to the plain grey
suit worn by the Iowa man.    Allerton and Nelson
were led to the stand by their grooms, and, as
the respective drivers, who were also the breeders,
owners, and trainers of the horses, took their
seats. the applause was deafening.    Nelson drew
the pole.    At the third score they are sent away,
with Nelson slightly in the lead, closely hugging
the pole.    At the first turn he has the advantage
of half a length.    At the quarter, which is reached in 32 seconds, Nelson has increased his lead to a
length.    Up the back stretch, Nelson goes very
fast, but the Iowa stallion keeps his place a
length in the rear, and they pass the half in 1:05¼,
in the same position.    Nelson now began to urge

his flying stallion, and as they reached the second turn, his lead was increased two lengths. Williams eased Allerton going round the turn. The three-quarter pole was passed in 1:39½. On straightening into the stretch, Allerton came on at a clip that was rapidly diminishing the distance between himself and Nelson. The crowds in the Amphitheatres were on their feet watching the result with breathless interest. At this critical moment, Allerton broke, and although he settled quickly, Nelson was at the distance stand, three lengths in the lead, when he got on his stride. Nelson looked around and swung his whip over his head in triumph, but found it necessary to use it on the back of his flagging steed before he reached the wire. Allerton came on with an electrical burst of speed and was only a half length behind as they finished in 2:13.

In spite of Nelson's winning the first heat, Allerton was still the favorite in the pools, bringing $25 against $17 for Nelson. They are off at the first score in the second heat. Nelson drives his horse at the limit of his speed and passes the quarter in 32¼ seconds, half a length ahead of Allerton. Going up the back stretch Nelson increased his lead, and as he passed the half in 1:06, Allerton is a length in the rear. Allerton closes up some of the gap going around the turn, and at

the three-quarter, which is reached in 1:41¼, he is
again but a length behind.   As they come into the
stretch Nelson increases his lead to two lengths.
At the distance stand Nelson swerved directly in
Allerton's path.   It was only the beginning of the
end.   Nelson tried to rally his tiring horse with a
vigorous use of the whip, and for a short distance
he showed a wonderful brush, but the clip was too
much for him, and when Allerton collared him
twenty yards from the wire he had had enough,
and Allerton won in the last few yards by half a
length, in 2:14½, in one of the finest finishes ever
witnessed.   Intense excitement prevailed and pro-
longed cheers greeted the winner.

Before the third heat Allerton brought $25 to
$6 for Nelson.   That Nelson has for a short dis-
tance a greater flight of speed than any horse on
the turf, was demonstrated in the third heat.
They are given the word for this heat with Nelson
half a length in advance, and going at a much
faster rate than Allerton.   Before reaching the
turn he has taken the pole, not, however, without
a palpable foul as he pulled in front of Allerton,
so that Mr. Williams had to take his horse back.
Nelson is at the quarter in 32 seconds, with Allerton moving along easily three lengths in the rear.
'Look at him!   Look at him!' cried Nelson's
friends. as on he sped, increasing his lead at every

stride. 'Why, he's simply playing with Allerton.' But they forgot that he was racing with a horse who does not know what it is to give up, and who always goes the last quarter of the mile the fastest. Mr. Williams rated Allerton along easily; and some idea of the lead Nelson had obtained may be formed when it is stated that Nelson passed the half mile pole in 1:05¼, Allerton passing the same point in 1:07½. Nelson goes to the three-quarter pole in 1:40, and still Allerton has made no play for the heat. Even his friends begin to get a little nervous as they noticed the long lead of the Maine stallion. But coming down the home stretch the brown colt strikes a 2:00 gait, and as he comes up to Nelson it is all over; he passes him as though he were going the other way. Mr. Williams eases him up and he wins by three lengths in a jog; time, 2:15. No pools were sold before the fourth heat. In the previous heat Nelson wore blinds, but he came out this time rigged as usual with an open bridle. Mr. Williams allows Nelson to set the pace, and they pass the quarter on even terms in 33½; up the back stretch they go like a double team, and as they pass the half in 1:07¼ it looks to the uninitiated like a pretty race; the three-quarter pole is reached in 1:42. At the distance Allerton begins to draw away. Nelson calls on his horse, but he has no brush left,

seeing which Williams pulls up, and Allerton takes
the heat in a jog in 2:16½, winning the race and
the largest purse ever won by a trotting horse.
The wildest excitement ever witnessed on a race
track ensued.    The air is filled with flying
cushions, hats, etc., and the applause is deafening.
Allerton is presented with an elegant floral offer-
ing in the shape of a full-sized blanket of cut
roses.    It was the most beautiful token imaginable.    The donors were Mr. and Mrs. Hull, who
presented it with the compliments of the Amul
Ree Stock Farm.    The time made in this race
will be something of a surprise and disappointment, but the day was not favorable, being cool
and cloudy, and the track is by no means the
fastest in the world.    Mr. Williams gave Allerton
as easy a race as possible, and it was evident that
he could have gone much faster every heat.    C.
H. Nelson owes C. W. Williams an everlasting
debt of gratitude for not humiliating him and
making a show of his horse in the fourth heat, and
in not doing so in view of all the circumstances
surrounding the case, and the previous talk of
Nelson, Mr. Williams displayed a magnanimity
hardly to be expected.

This performance should settle the question between the two great stallions.    While Nelson may
be able to show a greater flight of speed for a short

distance than the great Allerton, he cannot stay and trot a long drawn out race in fast time. Nelson, without doubt, is a great horse, but Allerton, the son of Jay Bird. is a greater.

## CHAPTER XIII..

### 1HE KIND OF A TROTTER TO OWN.

Immediately after his victory at Grand Rapids, Allerton was shipped to Lexington, Kentucky, to fulfill his engagement with Nancy Hanks at that place on the 15th of October.

No sooner had the great stallion arrived on the grounds than, strange to say, the Happy Medium mare was taken suddenly ill.

This was a sore disappointment to Mr. Williams, as he was anxious to meet the mare and give Allerton an opportunity to again try conclusions with her.    Mr. Doble suggested that as Mr. Williams had made the journey and the mare was not in condition to start, that he would substitute Delmarch, 2:11½, in her stead.    This Mr. Williams at first refused to do, but finally consented.

To outsiders this looked an easy race for Allerton, and such it proved to be.    But developments just before the start go a long way to show that the favored ones thought that under the skilfull hand of Doble, the little bay stallion could vanquish the king. There are times when the pool-box is a good indicator. The Horseman gives a short account as follows:

"The event of the day was the special. In last night's pooling Allerton was the favorite, selling for $1,000 to $650 for Delmarch. When the race was called, after the first heat in the pace, there were 25,000 people present. All the available space in both stands was taken, thousands in the infield, while the speculators were content to be in front of the stand, that they might have easy access to the box. Delmarch drew the pole and went to the post on even terms, and some pools sold with Delmarch the favorite, at $100 to $90. He was inclined to break before the start. They got the word on the fifth score. Doble set the pace. Williams laid on his wheel with the king and came the mile with ease. Doble called on Delmarch at the distance. Allerton was now on even terms, and soon was in the lead. Delmarch failed to respond. He was not the same horse as at Cambridge City or Terre Haute. He did not respond; he was beaten. The son of Jay Bird was sure the king of racing stallions. He was never urged, winning with seeming ease and speed to spare in 2:13¼.

Delmarch stock took quite a tumble, as every-one wanted to get their money on Allerton, and he sold for $50—and the wise.speculators could not get enough of it, while the suckers bought Del-march.

The only chance Allerton had to lose was to fall down.  The next heats were without incident, as Allerton took the lead from the word; Delmarch could not get to his wheel, and they were easy heats for the great stallion.

The applause was long and  loud, and many a warm and enthusiastic hand-shake did C. W. Wil-liams receive.  He was a proud man.  He looked it as he dismounted from his seat and was sur-rounded by the vast throng that gathered to be near the great stallion, and to see and shake the hand of the man who had bred and trained two of the greatest stallions known to the present age."

Allerton is quite a source of revenue to his owner.  Here, in less than two weeks, his winnings amount to $18,000, and no entrance fees.  That's the kind of a trotter to own.

The race at Lexington practically concluded Allerton's turf career for the season of 1891.  He was driven a few easy miles at the Independence fall meeting in 2:11 or 2:12, but was not asked to go fast again during the season. Allerton went into winter quarters at the close of the season of 1891 a better horse than he ever was before, and his prospects for the season of 1892 are the brightest.

Arrangements have been made for these two giants of the turf, Allerton and Axtell, to meet at Rush Park. Independence, Iowa, in August of 1892, and trot for a purse of $10,000 all to go to the winner. It will be worth a journey of thousands of miles to witness the contest. For, bear in mind, there will be no pulling in this affair, *it will be a horse race.*

And now, dear reader, we have about fulfilled our mission. Suffice it to recount in a few words the grand result attained by this prince of all horsemen, C. W. Williams. The first two colts ever foaled his property have accomplished the following:

One at three years of age was driven to a record of 2:12, · the world's stallion record, and was sold for $105,000. The other is, at five years of age, by all conceded to be the greatest race horse the world has ever seen, with a record of 2:09¼. and for him was offered $200,000.

These horses command a service fee of $1,000 each. Not more than six trotting horses in the world command so high a price, and these are two of them.

As a parting salute, I adjure you, see the great Allerton and Axtell race in 1892.

"All hail to regal Allerton!
  The king is on his throne;
For power and pluck and speed combined
  He simply stands alone.

A race horse! yes, from wire to wire:
  Majestic, perfect, grand,
He stands without a par on earth
  In any clime or land."

# J. W. MERCER,

## Original, Eclectic, Reformation Trainer.

---

### DRIVER OF INCAS, 2:14½

---

## INDEPENDENCE, IA.

---

# JOHN HUSSEY,

# TRAINER AND DRIVER,

## INDEPENDENCE, IOWA.

---

Special Attention Given to Handling and Developing Colts.

---

## STABLE AT RUSH PARK.

# EMPIRE HOUSE,

## INDEPENDENCE, IOWA.

---

Four Blocks from Rush Park.  Three Blocks from Post Office.

---

Good Sample Rooms.    Rates $2.00 Per Day.

---

### A. J. BOWLEY, Manager.

---

## "Breeding Investigated,"
## "Catalogues Compiled,"
## "Pedigrees Tabulated,"
## "Terms Reasonable."

---

WRITE FOR PRICES AND SAMPLE OF WORK, TO

### HILLIS ADY,

**Atalissa, Iowa.**